MW00882630

HABITS, HOSTS
AND THE
HOLY GHOST

Tales From A Catholic School Girl

KATHY WORMHOOD

BALBOA.
PRESS

A DIVISION OF HAY HOUSE

Balboa Press books may be ordered through booksellers or by contacting:

Balboa Press
A Division of Hay House
1663 Liberty Drive
Bloomington, IN 47403
www.balboapress.com
1-(877) 407-4847

Because of the dynamic nature of the Internet, any web addresses or links contained in this book may have changed since publication and may no longer be valid. The views expressed in this work are solely those of the author and do not necessarily reflect the views of the publisher, and the publisher hereby disclaims any responsibility for them.

The author of this book does not dispense medical advice or prescribe the use of any technique as a form of treatment for physical, emotional, or medical problems without the advice of a physician, either directly or indirectly. The intent of the author is only to offer information of a general nature to help you in your quest for emotional and spiritual well-being. In the event you use any of the information in this book for yourself, which is your constitutional right, the author and the publisher assume no responsibility for your actions.

Any people depicted in stock imagery provided by Thinkstock are models, and such images are being used for illustrative purposes only. Certain stock imagery © Thinkstock.

Printed in the United States of America.

ISBN: 978-1-4525-7346-5 (sc)
ISBN: 978-1-4525-7347-2 (e)

Balboa Press rev. date: 5/10/2013

TABLE OF CONTENTS

1963 NEW SCHOOL, THE NUNS, THE FEAR, OH MY! 1

1963 D-DAY 8

1963 O'HARA THE SCARA 18

1964 RUBBER IN THE ROAD 28

1964 DON'T MAKE THE ANGELS CRY 41

1964 SOUTH PAW 57

1965 BUBBLER AND BAZOOKA 67

1966 SPRING CLEANING FOR MARY 80

1967 RED ROVER, RED ROVER 87

1967 RECESS IS FOR KIDS 95

1968 SPRING SURPRISE 99

1968 NEVER ENOUGH BLESSINGS 107

1968 THE MAY PROCESSION 112

1968 A CLOSE CALL 119

1969 CHOIR PRACTICE 126

1969 A FLYING NUN AND A MONK 138

1969 LETTERS TO HOME 147

1969 BLESS ME FATHER 154

1969 REPORT CARD TIME 161

1969 THE SPEECH 173

1970 THE BIRD 180

1970 FORGET THE TWIRL!! 190

1971 THE JIG IS UP 197

1971 GOPHER 205

1971 CHANGES 214

1971 GRADUATION 227

1971 THE LAST DANCE 245

INTRODUCTION

There are certain experiences in your life that you look back on years later and see with completely different eyes. Experiences that were perhaps once scary now appear quite comical. My memories of attending a New England Catholic school are just like that. For years I recalled all the interesting stories of the nuns. And for years I blamed those same nuns for perhaps some of my own phobias and fears. But now, forty years later, I can see the humor in those experiences—and now I'm not afraid to talk about it!

Attending a parochial school was much different in the 1960's than it is in 2013. Those Sisters taught from a place of fear, guilt and shame. As little kids we respected them, or some of us did, but we walked around with fear and guilt. We were taught to listen to the nuns and hold the priests to a high standard for he was representing God. Like dutiful little soldiers we did as we were told and believed every word the nuns said. Most parents, mine included, trusted the nuns and believed the Catholic education was the best to receive, and maybe it was in certain aspects. The humorous stories written here are my own experiences and those of friends and family who also had the pleasure of learning from those Sisters, the priests and the rigid discipline at parochial school.

1963 NEW SCHOOL,
THE NUNS, THE FEAR, OH MY!

I was incredibly shy. Realistically, I was scared out of my wits. 1963 was a big year for me as I finished kindergarten and focused on September when I would be entering St. Timothy's Catholic School situated all the way across town. I knew about the gigantic brick school where the teachers were nuns and students wore matching outfits, because I used to see the classes as they filed into church. Some of my kindergarten friends were attending a public school. I didn't know what that meant at the time but my parents insisted I attend the Catholic one.

They told me the public education system only created hoodlums.

The oldest of a tight knit Irish Catholic family living in New England, I was expected to be the perfect, well behaved, quiet little girl. I was taught by my parents to go to church as often as possible, say my prayers, respect adults and be seen but not heard. I had no voice, no opinion, in the matter of where I would attend school.

In kindergarten I felt secure with my tiny group of friends at Bowman Street School, located just a few blocks from my house. My teacher, Mrs. Spencer was the best. She kept us busy everyday with lots of fun activities. The perky woman greeted us cheerfully each morning. I couldn't take my eyes off of the blood red lipstick highlighting the bright smile that graced her pale wrinkled face each day. She was like a sweet grandmother to each one of us.

That summer as I played in the neighborhood, I heard the older kids talking and laughing about their days at St. Timothy's which made me think Catholic school was nothing like kindergarten. They joked all the time about the crows and penguins. The group shared colorful tales of their day-to-day experiences with the Sisters. Over and over again they warned me to stay in the nuns' good graces. They said the worse thing anyone could do was get on their bad side or make them angry. But when I asked them what they meant, they roared with laughter and said, "You'll find out soon enough!"

It made me wonder. And whenever I questioned my mother about the crows she simply shrugged it off and said, "Oh, don't listen to those kids."

As the summer wore on my mother sensed my trepidation and tried her best to prepare me for my upcoming first day at St. Timothy's.

"Maureen Mary Mulldoon, there's nothing for you to worry about!" she said as she waved her hand in the air as if she were swatting a fly.

Every day she rambled on excitedly about the cute plaid uniforms I would be wearing and all the new friends I would meet. Over dinner she reiterated the privilege of the Catholic education I would be receiving and all the important things I would learn—things, I supposed, I would need for when I became a nun one day. After all, that seemed to be the ultimate goal—for me to devote my life as a nun.

She also told me how special it would be when I began to receive sacraments, especially First Holy Communion. On and on she babbled.

But I wasn't buying it. None of it alleviated my apprehension of starting at the new school.

Even at a young age I recognized that my mother skirted around any discussion of the Sisters of the Blessed Sacrament, the order of nuns who taught at the school and the reputation they had. But I didn't bother to question her because I knew she would ultimately give me a vague answer. So all summer long I relied on the rumors and scary stories I heard from the neighborhood kids.

By late August I was more anxious than ever. My one and only salvation was that my best friend, Ellen Callahan, would be starting first grade with me. She laughed at the stories of the nuns and wasn't the least bit nervous about school. Ellen lived right around the corner and we were like two peas in pod. The only difference was she had no desire to become a nun. Her family didn't pressure her towards the vocation because they were not as devout as my own. They went to church now and again, but not nearly as much as my mother did.

For as long as I could remember my mother and my Irish grandmother had insisted, coaxed and prayed novenas for me to enter the convent. Grammy Fitzpatrick reminded me many times over that she'd offered up rosaries to the Blessed Mother and lit candles for my vocation. I had no idea what becoming a nun would mean, but the two of them made it sound very special.

My grandmother's ancestors hailed from County Kerry Ireland and throughout the years many of the children in the family had dedicated their lives to the church. Her Irish relatives were proud of the boys that chose the priesthood and the many females who gave their lives to Christ. From the stories that were told the entire extended family held those devotees in high esteem—believing they themselves would get a free pass to heaven.

I knew the pressure was on.

That summer my curiosity grew and I began to observe the Sisters during Sunday mass. Each week the cluster of women could be seen in the same area, lined up rigidly in the front pew. I tried to imagine myself, as an adult, sitting there with them. But I was scared. I didn't want to be called a crow or a penguin. Many nights I dreamt I was dressed in the full nun garb when suddenly I was being chased by little children as they teased me and shouted Penguin!

As my mother tucked me into bed each night she smoothed my curls as she whispered into my ear.

"I can't believe my little girl is growing up."

And with a squeeze on my shoulders she'd say, "Don't you worry about those nuns or the new school."

I wanted her to be right. I prayed she was right. For good measure, just before falling off to sleep, I stared at the miniature crucifix hanging over my bedroom door and spoke directly to the man on the cross. Whispering to myself, I prayed that He would put Ellen and me together in the same classroom. And I prayed that all this worry about the nuns was for nothing.

On some weekends, my grandmother and I watched movies together about nuns: *The Bells of St. Mary's* with Ingrid Bergman and Bing Crosby, and *The Song of Bernadette* with Jennifer Jones. The nuns were beautiful; their faces serene. Grammy's encouragement and the touching stories motivated me to take that same path. But at church I began to notice that the local Sisters looked quite different than those in the movies. Each of them was encased in the drab black fabric from head to toe, with floor length habits and long veils. I watched their every move as they somberly returned to their seats after receiving Holy Communion. Their faces looked pained in their snug white headpieces. Some wore glasses; but not one of them wore lipstick or cosmetics of any kind. Not a strand of hair was visible around their bland pale faces.

These nuns looked nothing like Ingrid or Jennifer.

There was a time at church when I caught a glimpse of one of them with the slightest, barely noticeable smile. It was on Christmas morning. Mass had ended and I was leaving church with Grammy Fitzpatrick. I held tightly to her gloved hand as we met one of the nuns at the side door. Grammy paused and smiled cheerfully at the surly looking Sister.

"Merry Christmas, Sister" Grammy said in her heavy Irish brogue, nodding her head.

"Merry Christmas," the nun whispered. The brief curve to her lips lasted a second.

I clung to Grammy's hand as I watched the stiff-lipped nun tuck her hands into her wide sleeves, bow her head and continue to glide across the church driveway speaking to no one else. Even on Christmas Day that nun didn't look the least bit merry.

Unfortunately, the nuns weren't my only concern. My trepidation of Catholic school was also enhanced by my overprotective mother who worried about everything.

We lived in a quaint safe New England town where everybody knew everybody. But even so, on any given afternoon, as I played outside, my mother's ever watchful eyes were on me. And when I walked the short distance to Ellen's house just around the corner, I'd turn around to find my mother cautiously monitoring me. She'd stand in our driveway, my younger brother balanced on her hip, watching me as I approached Ellen's front door. If I wasn't already concerned about my safety, her behavior was causing me to be. And when it was time for me to head home Mrs. Callahan phoned my mother to let her know I was leaving. Rain or shine my mother stood outside to watch me come home. As a youngster there was never a time when I played outside without the presence of my worrisome mother cautiously observing my every move. At a very young age I began to wonder if I was ever going to be capable of doing anything on my own. Over time my mother's extreme nervousness caused me to question my own independence.

The summer flew by much too quickly. Daily trips to the lake kept Ellen and me busy and my mind off the nuns. When the Elks carnival came to town, I knew the halfway point was over and school was approaching way too fast. Fear began to consume me. I prayed and prayed that the stories I heard about Sisters of Blessed Sacrament were just that—stories.

1963 D-DAY

The dreaded day arrived and I had to face my fear.

On one unusually hot and humid August morning my mother drove to St. Timothy's to register me for first grade. During the ride my entire body felt clammy, not just from the weather, but from the anxiety building inside of me. As I thought about the nuns I would be meeting I could feel my heart thumping in my chest and my mouth became very dry. Despite the breeze coming in through the open car windows there was no escaping the humidity and I could feel my red hair curl with every passing minute.

I gazed out the window and thought about the friends from kindergarten who I wouldn't see again because they would be entering first grade at the public elementary school. And I wondered if they were scared or if any of them would grow up to be hoodlums.

My mother's Catholic school mantra played in my head as we drove down Main St. I knew it was extremely important to my parents, especially my devout mother, that I attend a parochial school. She believed blending religion with our education was the best way to raise her children, perhaps propelling us to our own religious vocation.

During the drive my mother nervously chatted on and on. She told me everything she knew about Sister Mary Xavier and Sister Mary such- and -such. My mind began to spin. Why did they all have names that started with Sister Mary? I could only hope that they should be as beautiful and sweet as Mary, the Blessed Virgin Mother.

We parked beside the church and walked down the driveway to the school's front entrance, located on Church St. I clenched a tiny wad of my mother's yellow flowered dress and struggled to keep up with her fast pace. Her pumps click-clacked on the pavement and I had to skip now and again to stay beside her. My clammy fist held tight to the cotton fabric as we climbed the steep granite steps of the school.

I wasn't about to let go.

One of the wide double doors was propped open and we stepped inside finding the principal's office just to the right of the foyer. Four classrooms lined either side of the long hallway, all of the doors were open and I could hear the murmuring of voices. When my eyes adjusted to the dark corridor, I took a double-take at the life-sized statue of Jesus that greeted us from the far end of the hall. The display was so real, as though He would come alive and begin speaking at any moment.

My mother squeezed my hand as she smoothed my curls then scooted me in front of her as we entered the office.

"Good morning, Sister."

She spoke softly to the nun who was seated at an enormous wood desk.

We took another tiny step just inside the door. The dismal room was full of stuff. Books and papers were stacked everywhere. Boxes covered student desks that were scattered about the room in no particular order. The office smelled musty, like old wet newspapers. Three large paned windows along the outside wall faced Messer St and were streaked and cloudy and needed a good washing. In the muted sunlight that filtered in I watched tiny dust particles float in the air. Sister Mary Xavier's desk sat in the corner of the room. It was completely covered with manila file folders, pencils and papers.

The place was a mess. It made me nervous and uneasy and I began to fidget as I looked around the office.

A three foot crucifix hung on the wall opposite the windows. I wondered what Jesus thought as he looked down upon the cluttered room. To the right of Him was a large round clock and I listened to the ticking of each second that went by.

My mother tightened her grip on my hand, cleared her throat and spoke once again.

"Excuse me, Sister."

I looked sheepishly over at Principal Xavier who appeared deep in thought. Her head was bowed to her chest. She might have been dozing, I couldn't tell.

A pen in her hand rested on a sheet of paper. Suddenly she cleared her throat and glanced over at us.

She was a very fat nun who completely filled the oak desk chair. Her face was squished by the white casing surrounding it and the wimple on her forehead pressed down causing horizontal wrinkles in her pale skin. A long black veil covered the white fabric on top of her head and continued down her back.

"Yesssss, yesssss. How can I help you?"

When she spoke her breath whistled through her teeth and she sounded like a hissing snake. She flung the pen down in agitation and turned in her chair to face us.

Her presence was intimidating.

The nun's gold cross glistened in the sun as it lay against the round white bib that covered her chest and shoulders. The sunlight reflected lots of peach fuzz on the sides of her chubby face and when she looked over her wire rimmed glasses I saw that her eyes were the brightest blue. But that was the only thing about her that was bright. Long gray straggly eyebrow hairs hung down touching the frame of her glasses. The sides of her mouth turned down as she scowled at us.

My mother pressed on.

"I'm here to register my daughter, Maureen, Maureen Mulldoon. She'll be entering first grade in September."

I had the feeling my mother felt intimidated by the nun. Her hands shook and she bit her lower lip as she released my hand and began to fumble with her shiny vinyl pocketbook. She nervously pulled out several crumpled tissues before finding the paper forms and gently set them on the corner of Sister's desk. Sister Xavier snatched the papers and began to review them. Sensing my mother's own anxiety, I became a little more nervous as I stood silently, watching and waiting. It was very warm and stuffy in the room and I could feel my cheeks flush. I grabbed another handful of my mother's dress and stood shyly behind her left leg.

"I believe everything is filled out correctly."

My mother took a step towards the huge desk.

Sister silently raised her hand in the air indicating my mother to stay put.

"Ssssso are you ready to ssstart ssschool, missss?"

As Sister Xavier's eyes focused on me I swallowed the lump in my throat and nodded.

"Sssspeak up, child! Sssspeak up when Sssissster is talking to you."

My mother put her hand on the small of my back and gently ushered me in front of her.

I thought I might throw up.

"Go ahead, Maureen, tell Sister."

"Yes, yes I am Sister."

The nun tossed my forms on top of a heaping stack of papers that was teetering on her desk then slowly stood up. As she adjusted the wide leather belt around her paunchy waist I watched the thick strand of wooden rosary beads sway and bounce against the desk.

"Well, then, let'sssss show you around ssschool. Follow me."

I reached up and held tight to my mother's hand. We turned to let Sister Xavier pass then we followed her out into the hall. I could hear her breathing, heavy and wheezy. Walking safely behind, I stared at the back of her waddling body and wondered if she might drop to the floor any minute.

The floors were gleaming from a recent polish and they creaked at times as we walked down the corridor. The mahogany walls glistened, and I could smell the blend of lemon polish and Lestoil. Sister pointed out the girls' lavatories.

"You mussst asssk permission before leaving your classsroom to go to the lavatory," she instructed, not waiting for a response.

Just then two young nuns whisked out of one of the classrooms and walked towards us.

"Good morning" they said in unison as they nodded to my mother and Sister Xavier.

I felt invisible.

I turned around to watch the two continue down the corridor. Their long black dresses, or habits, completely covered them. The black veils billowed out on the sides as the two women glided quickly and quietly down the hall. They looked completely identical from the back.

When I turned back around, I caught sight of the Jesus statue at the end of the hall. It was as though He was looking directly at me as we headed in His direction. I never took my eyes off of it. Sure enough, Sister led us right to Him, toward one of the classrooms just to the left. My heart fluttered a little as we approached the statue and I squeezed my mother's hand even tighter. Just before entering the room I stole a glance to His face.

His piercing eyes seemed to look directly into mine. His hands had painted blood and wounds on the palms. He was as tall as my Dad, maybe even taller. Painted yellow and orange robes were faded as they flowed down to His sandaled feet. I instinctively leaned in to my mother and away from the statue as we entered the classroom.

"Sssissster, here issss another new sssstudent of yoursss."

Sister Mary Dympna was at the back of the classroom placing cardboard cutouts of the alphabet across the wall. She put down her work and came to greet us. Well, she actually greeted my mother, not me.

"Good morning, I'm Sister Dympna."

The stout nun waddled between the desks. She managed a smile at my mother then peered down her hooked nose at me.

"Good morning." My mother responded cheerfully.

"Maureen, say hello to Sister."

"Hello."

The nun's face was not very friendly so I cast my eyes to the floor. Her cold demeanor made me feel as though I didn't exist or didn't belong there.

"She's a shy one, isn't she?" Sister Dympna asked my mother. "Well, that'll change once she starts school. And Lord above! Would you look at that mound of messy curly hair!"

That was it. That's all she had to say to me. No welcome to St. Timothy's, no welcome to first grade.

With that she turned on her heel and continued hanging her cutouts.

Sister Xavier ushered us out of the classroom and we continued on our tour. The building was huge and I worried if I would ever find my way around. We ventured through a back hallway and down two flights of stairs. It was dark and scary in the back halls and I wondered where she was taking us. Would we find our way out?

When we reached the bottom of the staircase we came to a heavy white door. Sister pushed it open and we entered the brightly lit cafeteria. Long brown lunch tables filled the room.

"I don't know if she will be buying hot lunch but if sssso thisss isss where she will go."

Sister Xavier led us over to the food line. Rectangle stainless serving containers were empty and rested on top of several tables. Just behind the serving line was a large pass through in the wall. I could see two stoves and one enormous refrigerator. Three hefty ladies with tight hair nets and white aprons were busy in the kitchen. They waved to Sister then continued with their work. She of course, didn't wave back.

As we passed the serving tables I saw the gigantic pile of plastic lunch trays stacked neatly next to the bin full of silverware, ready to be used the upcoming school year.

All the while Sister continued to explain the process of buying a hot lunch every day.

As Sister Xavier led us through a hallway towards the gymnasium a man's deep voice startled me.

"Hello, Sister."

I looked up to see a tall lanky man dressed in a green work uniform. He was leaning against the doorway of what appeared to be a broom closet. Sister never acknowledged him. The man stood perfectly still and stared at us with a goofy sideways grin. He gave me the creeps.

"That was our janitor, Mr. Lachant. He's a little slow, but he's harmless."

Again I squeezed my mother's hand and hurried past the scary man as the nun brought us into the gymnasium. As we strolled through the empty space Sister's voice echoed as she described the many events that took place there. St. Timothy's Midgets, the boy's basketball team, played on Friday evenings. Both the Girl Scouts and Brownie troops held regular meetings in the gym. On the east side of the gymnasium was an enormous stage. Sister paused in front of it as she proudly described the variety shows that the students put on several times each year.

"Yesssss, everyone enjoysss our sssstudentssss' performancesss. Everyone isss involved ssso every child hasss a part in the show."

My mind began to wander. It sounded exciting and I wondered if I would be in a show.

We continued through a small alcove, up the back stairs and to the back door. Our tour ended outside in what Sister called the schoolyard. The nun stood with her arms crossed and tucked into her wide sleeves. Her breathing was labored after our walk around school.

"Do you have any questionsss?" she asked my mother.

My mother glanced down at me and quickly replied, "No, I don't think so, Sister. I really appreciate your time today."

It didn't matter. I wouldn't have asked any questions anyway.

"Well then, we shall sssee Misssss Maureen in Ssssseptember. God bless and good day Mrs. Mulldoon."

She turned and waddled back inside.

As my mother and I headed over to our car I scanned the schoolyard and realized it also doubled as the parking lot for the church next door. There was no swing set, slide or any fun equipment to play on. The entire space was pavement.

I climbed in the front seat of our '57 Ford, closed the door and turned to look back at my new school.

It was a foreboding two story brick building. I wondered if I would find my way or if I could get to the cafeteria. What if I couldn't find the lavatory?

My thoughts were interrupted.

Sister Mary Xavier's forehead was pressed against the window of the door we had just exited. I could have sworn she was looking directly at me. A shiver shot up my spine as I slouched lower in the seat.

But I kept the nun in my vision for as long as I could.

As far as I was concerned summer could go on forever.

1963 O'HARA THE SCARA

The O'Hara clan originated from Dungarvan, County Waterford, Ireland. As they settled in the small New England town, they pumped out children like candy from a Pez dispenser. At least that's what my grandparents said. The family was enormous with seven boys and five girls. Everyone in town knew of the O'Hara kids because they were always in trouble. Unfortunately, the parents' harsh discipline didn't affect their offspring. Mr. O'Hara had a stern hand and used his belt on both the boys and the girls. Mrs. O'Hara chose a wooden spoon to control her kids and whiskey to control her depression.

The boys were rebellious. As teenagers they ran wild in the small town and over the years the locals gossiped as illegitimate redheaded babies began to surface.

The O'Hara girls were tough as well. Most of them married local men and generated large broods of children. Only one girl, Colleen, escaped the cycle of the small town life. She entered a convent, became a nun and lived several states away.

As I was growing up I was told over and over again by both my parents and grandparents to stay away from the wild O'Hara children.

"They're nothing but trouble!" my mother would say.

She didn't have to tell me twice.

The thought of anyone's father using the belt gave me the shivers. And I didn't know either one of my parents to drink.

Steven Daniel O'Hara was the youngest of the well known brood and in 1963 he and I began first grade together at St. Timothy's. The nuns voiced dismay at the thought of teaching another O'Hara offspring.

"He's sure to be just like his siblings!" was the comment I heard by the school principal.

And they were right.

From day one the Sisters of the Blessed Sacrament had their work cut out for them with Steven. Always mischievous, he kept the nuns on their toes. Just hearing his colorful language caused the nuns to visibly cringe whenever they saw the young ruffian approaching.

With my mother's voice echoing in my head I tried to keep my distance from him. How could anyone be so stupid to do something to irritate the nuns? Everyone knew how strict they were.

Most of us did whatever it took to stay out of their line of fire and avoid their punishment. But nothing fazed Steven. Even at the tender age of six he had the gumption to try anything to stir up some excitement.

On one particular October morning our entire first grade class truly believed Steven O'Hara had killed our teacher, Sister Mary Dympna.

Earlier that morning my mother had dropped Ellen and me off on the corner of Church St. right in front of school. Normally, we met up with Steven each day as he walked up from Canal Street, coming from the complete opposite direction. I had no idea where he lived but somehow we met him at the same spot every morning. The boy was always by himself even though I knew he had loads of older brothers and sisters. But Steven was always alone both before and after school. I noticed some days he looked lonely as he walked by himself and I wondered where the rest of his family was. I didn't even know what they looked like. Even though we were both Catholic I never saw Steven with his family at Sunday Mass. I thought about his parents and if they ever went to church.

That particular morning the sidewalks glistened from the rain the night before. Autumn leaves, pine needles and plenty of worms floated in random puddles on the side of the road. I became annoyed as I watched Steven in front of us. He constantly stepped off the sidewalk to scoop up a stone, pinecone or other object of interest. Why can't he behave and stay on the sidewalk like the rest of us, I thought. The street was bustling with early morning traffic. Suddenly he shouted, "Hey little guy!!"

He jumped from the edge of the sidewalk onto the busy street without even looking for oncoming cars. He ran halfway across the road and picked something up as vehicles began to blow their horns. I stopped in my tracks and watched the foolish boy.

"Mulldoon, look!!"

Steven ran towards me and stuck his newfound treasure under my nose. It was the biggest, ugliest brown bullfrog I had ever seen.

"Ew! Get that slimy thing out of here!"

I reeled backwards. I wasn't afraid of the frog but everyone knew that they caused warts if they touched your skin.

"Put him down Steven! You're gonna end up with warts!"

"Don't be such a goddamned scaredy cat Mulldoon!!"

His language always shocked me.

Steven proudly carried the dirty frog into school. As we climbed the front steps I watched as he shoved the amphibian into his front pocket. When he leaned over and yanked on my book bag I heard him whisper, "I'm gonna scare the shit outta Sister Dympna! I hope the old fricken crow gets warts all over her goddamned face!"

Since we just entered school, I didn't have a chance to respond. All I knew was that Steven was the craziest boy I'd ever met. He had a lot of guts. But I couldn't help but wonder what his parents thought of him using all those bad words all the time.

Things didn't go as planned.

After making sure the coast was clear and Sister was nowhere in sight, Steven wasted no time. He went straight to the nun's oak desk and pulled the frog out of his pocket.

It croaked loudly causing some of the students to become curious and they began to gather around him.

"Back the hell off!" the six-year-old ordered as he pulled out the nun's large wooden chair and placed the frog on the seat.

"Scram!" he shouted as he sprinted back to his own desk just in the nick of time.

As Sister Dympna entered the classroom I watched a stack of graded papers fly off the corner of her desk as all of the other students scurried away. Sister clapped her hands as she tried to get everyone's attention.

"Quiet children! Quiet!"

My heart pounded as I watched the nun slowly make her way to the front of the room. Sister Dympna was short and chubby with a hooked ruby red nose and pink flushed cheeks. She always looked as though she had just come in from a cold winter's day. Sister took her place just under the American flag. Her black veil and head piece brushed the edge of the red and white stripes.

"Please stand for the Pledge of Allegiance."

I looked up at the flag and placed my hand over my heart. Before we could utter the first word there was a loud croak.

RIIIIBBBBBIT!!

Sister snapped her head around as she tried to find where the noise was coming from. Her eyebrows knotted together as she scanned the room.

RIIIIBBBBBIT!!

Sister Dympna had the most quizzical look on her face as she slowly looked around.

None of us dared to move or say a word. Following the sound she leaned over and looked behind her desk then began to scream like a little girl.

"AAAHH!! AAAHH! OH MY GOD! OH MY LORD!"

Her reaction made me jump as she began to flail her arms in the air. Steven never anticipated her reaction. Stunned, we continued to stand with our hands on our hearts. All we could do was watch. My mouth dropped open and I didn't know whether to laugh or cry. Steven, the only daring one, covered his mouth attempting to muffle his laughter.

"Somebody get that thing OUT OF HERE!!!"

Sister's voice quivered and she began to visibly shake. My heart pounded in my chest, and I felt numb as I watched the frightened nun. Sister began to make soft whimpering noises as she backed into the blackboard, constantly wringing her hands. The girl next to me began to cry.

"Go get it!" I whispered loudly to Steven tugging on his shirt sleeve. "Hurry up before she starts crying or something!!"

His funny prank was spiraling out of control. Steven glanced over at me, and I could see the wheels turning. He was up to something. What on earth was he waiting for??

"Go, you idiot! Hurry up! It's not funny anymore!"

With a slight grin Steven sauntered to the front and leaned over the desk to look at the frog.

"It's just an innocent lil frog, Sister. Look, he aint' doin' nothin'"

"Take it awaaay! Take it awaaaay!"

Her voice was growing faint. Sister shook uncontrollably and her body became limp. Everything seemed to be happening in slow motion. She slid slowly down the chalkboard and looked as though she might pass out. Steven scooped the frog into his hand and covered it with the other. He stepped closer to Sister Dympna and held it up to her now ashen face. The frog was just under her nose.

"Seeeeee??"

"NOOOO! AAAHHH!"

"Touch it, Sister! Touch it! He ain't gonna hurt ya!"

Steven continued to taunt the petrified nun who slid all the way to the floor and landed with a thud. Her legs were open in a wide V and her head slumped to one side. Muffled sobs oozed from her pudgy lips. Steven stood there, dumbfounded. I covered my mouth as I gasped at the sight.

The nun's long bulky black habit was twisted up to just below her knees. Her thick legs were exposed like two tightly packed sausages bulging in her sheer black hose. Another inch or two and her garter belt would have been showing. The nun's left hand clutched the wooden cross of her mahogany rosary beads as though they were going to save her. Her entire face was squeezed by the white headpiece that she wore. The back of Sister's veil was caught on the chalk tray and I saw a glimpse of hair!

With wide eyes, Steven gulped as he stared at his victim.

Suddenly her legs began to twitch causing her head to slip lower onto her ample bosom. A thin strand of drool dripped onto her large white circular collar.

Steven took a step backward, never taking his eyes of the fallen nun.

"Oh shit" he whispered. "Oh shit, shit shit."

I made my way over to Steven.

"Oh my God, Steven!! What should we do?"

Two other boys came forward just then and looked down at Sister Dympna.

"Is she dead??"

"I think you killed Sister!!"

"No! She's not dead, you idiots!! Look at the drool!"

But I could tell that Steven was scared and was trying to convince himself.

Janie McMack, who was known as the teacher's pet, began to sob loudly when she overheard the boys' comments and ran screaming out of the room, "Sister's dead!! Sister Dympna's dead!!"

"Goddamned Janie!" Steven muttered.

But it was too late to go after her. Within seconds Sister Xavier scurried into the classroom.

"Move aside children! Move aside!"

She frantically waved her arms in front of her as she made her way through the group fixated on the nun.

Steven clutched the bullfrog and shoved it into his pocket.

"Sister Dympna! Sister, can you hear me? Oh Lord above help us!"

Sister Xavier grunted and groaned as she knelt beside our teacher. She gently tapped the nun's face finally wakening Sister Dympna.

"Thank you Jesus, Mary and Joseph!" Sister Xavier exclaimed as she helped the other nun to her feet.

Sister Dympna steadied herself, blinked her eyes several times then looked around the room.

Her eyes fell on her culprit. Amidst all of the chaos Steven had managed to make his way to the back of the classroom. Standing on his tiptoes he leaned across the radiator and with both hands he lifted the sash of a large window and tossed the frog outside. But when he spun around he was confronted by one very angry nun. Sister Dympna stood with her hands on her hips. Her recent ashen face was now beet red and she was breathing loud and heavy. Their faces were only inches apart.

Everyone watched anxiously. It was the moment of truth for Steven. I couldn't believe what happened next. The boy lost his composure as he tried to stifle a chuckle which only erupted into raucous laughter.

The sharp slap from Sister's hand startled all of us.

I squeezed my eyes shut for a second as the second strike snapped Steven quickly back to reality. He appeared to be dizzy and stunned from the slap.

A shiver ran up my spine.

The pink handprint lasted a day but the memory of it lasted years. From that day forward my trepidation of the

Catholic nuns increased tremendously. The movies never depicted such behavior.

And from that day on I saw Steven in a different light. He was the rebel that I never could be—a rebel who wasn't afraid of the nuns or anyone else for that matter—and he brought excitement to the classroom.

For the next three weeks Steven O'Hara stayed after the last bell.

As we filed out of the classroom the boy wore a broad smile as he clapped erasers out of the same window where the innocent little frog had escaped.

I knew the reason for his smile. He'd earned a new nickname.

From that day on everyone called him O'Hara the Scara.

1964 RUBBER IN THE ROAD

I was in second grade and was beginning to feel some freedom. My parents finally allowed me to walk to school with the other neighborhood kids, the 'big kids' we called them. And I was released from my mother's constant hovering. Since I was the oldest of the four Mulldoon children I was the one who had to set the precedent and break the ice for my younger siblings. However, whenever I tried to do so my mother became a nervous wreck. I encountered opposition each time I asked to do something that didn't include her. When I wanted to go on a hike to the valley with Ellen she fretted. And when I wanted to go on a picnic in the woods right in back of our home she voiced concern.

"Oh, I don't know Maureen, should you be doing that? What if there are wild animals?"

It was frustrating.

I hoped that walking to school with my friends would give me some independence, even in a small way.

My sheltered mother had been born and raised in the small New England town, never traveling much outside the city limits. Dad was brought up 40 miles away, out in the country where his family ran a profitable dairy farm. Just months after they met at a county fair, he and my mother married. It was his decision to settle in town. Memories of his country life were filled with long school bus rides each day and missing out on fun times with classmates after school and Dad wanted more for his own children.

But his choice resulted in an occupation other than the farm, requiring him to work two, sometimes, three jobs to provide for his growing family.

My mother was the typical housewife and undoubtedly an extremely devout Catholic. Each Sunday she woke us at the crack of dawn, scrubbed our faces and dragged all four of us kids to the 8:00 mass. And on every Holy Day of Obligation she insisted we all go to church, even if we had already attended while at school that day. My father, dog tired from working so many jobs, only went to what he called C and E, Christmas and Easter masses.

His absence each day left my mother to discipline us and run the household herself. On days when she was feeling extremely nervous my siblings and I learned to steer clear of her.

"Are you feeling okay? Let me take your temperature again."

We'd try to out run her, going round and round the dining room table as we escaped her ever present thermometer.

After breakfast each weekday morning I said goodbye to my mother, grabbed the tiny brown paper bag containing my lunch and prepared to dash out the kitchen door. I never made it without a hitch. Even with my younger siblings milling about the kitchen my mother managed to snag my loaded down book bag as she continued to stir the gigantic pot of oatmeal. I waited impatiently as she licked her fingers and proceeded to flatten my unruly curls.

"Lord, have mercy Maureen! We have to do something with this hair of yours!"

It didn't matter that I had combed them out each morning my hair inevitably retreated back to predictive spirals.

"I have to go ma!"

I managed to wriggle out of her grasp and dash outside.

Ellen waited for me at our designated spot each morning. We had decided to meet just outside the gates of Union Cemetery just across the street from my home. Both of us looked forward to school that year. We felt cool, grown up, as we were now allowed to walk with the older kids from the neighborhood. But there were rules I had to follow.

Each night I was given strict instruction from my father as he pointed his finger at me.

"Stay on the sidewalk!!" he demanded. "And stay with the other kids. Don't be walking by yourself!"

But though Dad's speech was stern he always ended with a warm bear hug and a huge grin under his auburn handlebar mustache.

On one damp morning in March I was running a little late. I nodded in agreement to my mother's ever insistent instructions as I struggled to put my red rubbers over my shoes.

I hated those red rubbers.

They made my almost seven-year-old feet feel gigantic and heavy. I was finally able to scoot out the door just in time to meet Ellen and the other kids. I felt clumsy with the weight of the rubbers but I managed to keep up with the group. I knew Chubby Billy would wait for no one.

Chubby's real name was William Holland, but everyone called him Chubby behind his back. A fat 14 year old boy who wore a pocket protector, bright white socks and his pants way too high, Chubby Billy was the supreme nerd. And because he was the oldest in our group he was also very bossy.

His family lived up the street from mine and his parents were much older. They actually reminded me of my grandparents. His father worked at the foundry and his mother was an expert seamstress.

One Saturday morning my mother needed assistance with a sewing project and arranged a visit with Chubby's mother. My mother, bless her heart, had been struggling as she tried her best to create sundresses for me to wear during summer vacation. I didn't want to go but she dragged me along so the measurements would be correct.

Mrs. Holland was a pale thin woman who I imagined never went out in the sun. As the two women sat at the kitchen table discussing the dress pattern, I stood quietly next to my mother as Chubby shuffled into the kitchen.

He didn't notice me until he turned from the refrigerator. I tried not to laugh but I'm sure he could tell by me face that I found something funny. Chubby Billy was still wearing his flannel pajamas. They were covered with cowboys and Indians and the bottoms were hiked up under his armpits.

He flashed me a dirty look and snapped, "Something funny Maureen?"

The two women glanced up at William then at me. I never said a word.

But after that incident Chubby had no tolerance for me. He barely looked or even spoke to me.

This day, just like any other, Chubby Billy was in his glory as he led our neighborhood group to school. He acted superior to us as he rambled on, to no one in particular, about his plans to become a teacher. I determined Chubby would certainly fulfill his dream. After all, he used big words all the time and liked to boss us younger kids around.

"Come on, come on!!" he barked as he quickly picked up the pace. Leading us down the sidewalk Chubby wove his way around muddy slush and puddles of melted snow. We followed him in single file, like little ducklings. A few of the others stomped and splashed their way through the slush; the wet sludge covering their feet and soaking their rubbers, shoes and legs.

Noticing that the kids were creating a mess with the snow Chubby announced over his shoulder "This is crazy! Follow me!!"

I watched in disbelief as he tromped a path through a small snow bank and stepped onto Academy Street. He knew it was wrong. I knew it was wrong. We were breaking one of the all important rules.

"I'm not supposed to go in the street!" I whispered to Ellen.

"But we have to stay together, come on." she called as she skipped ahead. "No one's going to find out!"

Everyone else followed him but I hesitated as I glanced behind me to be sure my mother wasn't watching or my father wasn't driving down the street. Then I took off running. Holding my green book bag tight to my chest I concentrated on catching up with my friends.

I don't know how it happened.

Before I knew it I was laying face first on the ground.

"Help!"

I yelled to the group as I saw my books scattered across the wet road. The damp ground was cold against my belly and my hands were sore and red from being scraped on the pavement.

Chubby Billy stopped and motioned to the others to wait as he trotted back to check on me.

"What happened? Get up Maureen!" he demanded. "Where the hell is your shoe?"

I cried softly as I sat up and looked at my feet. My left shoe and red rubber were missing. I quickly stood up and looked around. I limped on one wet sock as I frantically searched the area. I didn't see them anywhere. My book bag lay next to a grated manhole cover. I scooped it up and collected my books then I began to wail. Chubby stood and watched me.

"I don't knoooooow! Help meeeee, Williammmmm!"

"I don't have time for stinking cry babies! You'd better find it and get your ass to school! And you'd better not be late or you'll catch hell from Sister!"

And with that, Chubby turned on one heel and left me standing by myself.

I didn't know what to do next and I began to shiver uncontrollably. Ellen rushed to my side to help.

"What happened? Where's your shoe??"

"I don't know!! I don't know!!"

My friend and I spent the next several minutes looking along the side of the road. But the shoe was nowhere to be found. Ellen shrugged her shoulders and bit her nails.

"I have to go Maureen. I can't be late! You know how Sister Cornelius gets when anyone is late for school!"

She hurried to meet up with the others, who had now continued on their way. I couldn't get angry with her. I knew she had to get to school otherwise she'd risk being in trouble as well.

I limped around in a circle looking for my rubber covered shoe. I scooped out some snow from the small bank on the side of the street and looked in the middle of the road. Crying softly I returned to the sidewalk, confused as to what I should do next. Minutes later I heard a car pull up beside me. The hair stood up on the back of my neck. I worried it was a stranger.

"Maureen! What are you doing!?"

It was Mr. Patterson from our neighborhood. A friend of my father's, he was also the father of eight boys. When he got out of the car I began to cry even harder. Through sobs I tried to tell him what had happened. He looked around for my shoe and when we couldn't find it he said he had to bring me home. I was really scared. First I had broken a major rule by walking in the street, now I was found by myself, with no one else in sight.

Mr. Patterson walked me to the back door. When my mother saw us out the kitchen window she opened the door in a fury.

"What on earth are you doing here? Why aren't you on your way to school?"

Mr. Patterson explained all that he knew about my dilemma to my parents as I began to sob.

My mother yelled upstairs to my father, who was getting ready for work.

The two of them stood in the doorway staring at my shoeless foot.

"Okay, miss. You'd better start talking! What the hell happened?"

Afraid that I would get into big trouble I lied through my teeth.

"I tripped. And...and... then...my... shoe...fell...off!!" I sobbed.

I purposely ignored the fact that it all happened in the street.

My father thanked Mr. Patterson for his help, grabbed the keys to our Ford and the sleeve of my jacket as he ushered me to the car. I limped down the driveway, my stocking now thoroughly soaked.

"Okay, show me where it happened."

We drove to the spot where my fabricated story began. He pulled the car over and went immediately to the sidewalk. Up and down the pavement we walked. Minutes later it was obvious things were not adding up. My exasperated father took me by the shoulders and looked directly into my eyes.

"Maureen Mary Mulldoon! Something is not right here. You'd better tell me the truth!"

I sobbed uncontrollably, afraid of the repercussions. Then I slowly pointed to the street.

"Were you out in the street?"

I could only nod. Hyperventilation was setting in.

He climbed over the dirty snow bank and stood for a minute. Then he motioned for me to join him. I limped on my tiptoes and stood next to him.

"Show me what happened."

I began to walk slowly, stopping at the manhole cover.

"I found my book bag right here." I looked up at him with tearful eyes.

He lifted my chin and said softly "Didn't I tell you to stay on the sidewalk?"

His demeanor and soft eyes confirmed that he wasn't going to punish me. In fact I could tell he truly felt sorry for me. I nodded as I looked down at my feet, one red rubber still in place.

Suddenly Dad blurted, "Holy shit. Lookie there!"

We both peered down into the round hole. There it was.

My red rubber was floating in the sewer. It bobbed on top of the murky brown water just beneath the manhole cover.

"I'll be damned."

Dad scratched his head and looked around. Just up the street, on the corner of Lincoln and Academy several city workers were repairing the sidewalk. He grabbed my hand, and headed over to the group. I stood quietly and listened as he explained to them my story.

And after they stopped laughing the men agreed to help us.

I watched as one of the men lifted the heavy grated cover. Then with a long hooked pole he lifted my lonely shoe from the sewer.

But Dad wasn't cutting me any slack. As he drove me to school he made me wear the soggy thing.

Shame and embarrassment would have been enough punishment for me but I knew I still had to face Sister Cornelius. As we drove down Main Street I said a silent prayer that perhaps she might feel bad and have mercy on me.

But I was wrong. Out in the hall Sister slowly shook her head as she listened to my father's explanation. Her squinted eyes bore right through me causing my cheeks to burn with the sting of humiliation and guilt.

Throughout the day I had the constant reminder of the morning incident. Every time I took a step my foot was tight in my swollen water-soaked shoe. But I never said a word to anyone. Not even Ellen.

Just before the last bell rang that day Sister called me to her desk.

"Miss Mulldoon, please remain in your seat. Your father has given me permission to keep you after school today."

"Yes, Sister."

I bowed my head and returned to my desk. Crap. I had never been tardy to her class before and didn't think it could get me into that much trouble.

I watched as my fellow classmates left the room and headed home. When Ellen saw that I had to stay after class she gave me a quizzical look and a small wave before skipping out the door. I shrugged my shoulders and stayed at my desk, waiting for Sister.

In the quiet I heard a snicker, a sinister chuckle, coming from behind me.

Steven.

It was no surprise that he was staying after school. But why did it have to be that same day.

"What the hell did you do, Mulldoon? C'mon whatcha do?"

My back was rigid as I sat perfectly still trying to ignore his remarks. Sister was chatting out in the hall, and for once, I wished she'd hurry up and come back into the classroom.

I was determined to keep my secret.

"Come on! Fess up! Whatcha do?"

Steven was relentless but I remained silent. No one, especially O'Hara the Scara, could ever find out where my shoe had landed that day.

When she returned to the classroom Sister called the two of us to the front and instructed us to kneel in front of her desk. As the nun placed a math text book in each of our hands I glanced over at Steven whose face was calm, as though he'd been through this before.

"Extend your arms. And keep them there until I return."

I slowly raised both arms. The books were heavy and my little limbs quivered.

Steven bit his lower lip in defiance and kept his arms still and his eyes to the front. I tried, but the weight was too much and I let them drop to the floor. I glanced at the door hoping Sister didn't catch me. When I heard voices I managed to return to the outstretched position. My shoulders ached and my hands were tingling. The books felt like they would drop any second.

"Alright, put them down and come here."

For the next hour, under the watchful eye of Sister Cornelius, Steven and I wiped down the blackboards and cleaned the erasers.

My entire body felt lopsided as though I were standing on a thick engorged sponge. I tried not to limp because I knew Steven sensed that something was up. But anytime he tried to speak to me I was relieved Sister raised her hand demanding silence.

My lips would be forever sealed.

And my treks to school would now only be on sidewalks.

There was a lot to be learned in second grade.

1964 DON'T MAKE
THE ANGELS CRY

In November, 1964 my second grade class began a rite of passage. Our young minds had a lot to learn as we studied the two sacraments to be received that school year. The first was the sacrament of Penance, also known as confession. We practiced the Act of Contrition prayer over and over again—so much so, that some nights it played in my head as I drifted off to sleep. It was an important prayer that was required each time we went to confession.

Sister Cornelius reinforced to each one of us that we were born with original sin. I had no idea what I could have done but I believed her. Thankfully, she also said we could wash away those sins by visiting the confessional and telling the priest all that we had done wrong. The Sacrament of Penance was the stepping stone to the all important childhood sacrament, First Holy Communion. And in April 1965 we made our first confession during the Lenten period, just before Easter.

To prepare us for Holy Communion, Sister taught us about the Last Supper and the events leading up to it. We were told about the 12 apostles; the dedicated men who followed Jesus while He lived His life on earth. All were good and faithful followers except for two, Simon Peter and Judas, who eventually betrayed him. When Simon Peter heard the cock crow three times, he remembered the prediction Jesus had told him and he knew he was in trouble. And then there was Judas who wanted the 30 pieces of silver more than he wanted to protect his friend. But in the end he knew he had made a terrible mistake.

As a seven year old these were frightening stories. I knew I never, ever wanted to betray Jesus. And I absolutely knew I wanted to go to heaven. So I listened intently and tried to absorb Sister's every word.

Sister Cornelius explained to us the importance of receiving the host, the pale round wafer she called the body of Christ.

"At each Mass, the priest consecrates the host and the wine, turning them into the body and blood of our Lord."

The body and blood....I was not so sure it was something I wanted to taste. But Sister Cornelius assured us it was the holy thing to do. Doing so would bring us closer to God, she said, and get us into heaven. As time went on I tried not to think of Sister's description and concentrated on the benefits of partaking in the Eucharist.

Once a week we practiced the ritual of communion in our classroom. Sister reviewed the lengthy liturgy that

Father Murphy would be reciting during the ceremony. And since it was customary to kneel during the Eucharist, the nun forced us to kneel beside our desks. The wood floor was hard, and my bony knees hurt but Sister reminded us of how much Jesus had suffered, so I bowed my head and folded my hands in prayer, as I tried to ignore the pain.

Sister stood behind her desk as she played the role of Father Murphy at the altar. Holding a tall glass of water between her hands she began to recite some prayers.

"Jesus raised the cup and said take this and drink from it, for this is my blood. Now remember children, Father will be saying these prayers in Latin but I want you to know what they mean."

I was glad to finally understand. Each Sunday Father said the entire mass in Latin. I swore he mumbled because I could never understand him and always became fidgety and bored. My mind wandered during the hour long Mass as I tried to take in everything the priest did. He stood with his back to us at the large rectangle table located on the altar and even if I stood on the vinyl kneeler, I couldn't see everything he was doing up there. Wearing a floor length black robe, or vestment, with a white overlay across his shoulders he looked like a magician performing tricks as he raised and lowered his arms and recited prayers in the funny language. I could see the shiny cup he held up and the large white thing that looked like a giant cookie. Periodically, Father bowed to the table. It was all very mysterious.

Sister raised the cup in front of her face.

"This is when the altar boy will ring the bells. Make sure you bow your heads to show your reverence to our Lord."

As each of us bowed our heads to our chest I wondered how long we were to stay there and glanced up at Sister just as she set the glass down and continued.

"Just bow your heads for as long as the bells ring."

Next, she held up a circular cutout from a brown paper bag. It was intended to represent the consecrated host the priest blessed each Sunday. Sister Cornelius raised the round paper in front of her forehead and said, "Take this and eat it. This is my body. The bells will ring again, so please bow your heads once more."

Everyone was silent as we did what the nun instructed. After she finished she paired us up to practice the ceremonial walk to church. As luck would have it, I had to walk with Steven.

"I can't wait to make my First Communion." he whispered to me. "I'm always famished at mass. After this I'll be able to fill up on the host! I just hope the goddamned thing tastes good."

I turned away as I tried to ignore his flippant comments. Didn't he see that Sister was right in the room? The boy made jokes about everything. First Communion was a sacred sacrament and he had no problem making fun of it. Sister pinned tissues on all the girls' heads then we quietly exited the classroom.

"Hands together, children. Fold your hands in prayer."

Sister Cornelius held the front door open allowing each of us to pass by for her inspection. Francis O'Neal, the tallest boy in class, and his partner, teacher's-pet-and-goody-two-shoes-all-rolled-into-one Janie McMack had been instructed to lead us as far as the driveway to the church. Sister gave Janie a cheery smile as she watched the girl lead the procession but her smile quickly disappeared as she gave the rest of us the once over.

If the Sisters of St. Timothy's believed Steven listened only to the devil, they acted as though Janie's ears heard angels' voices. Trouble never visited her. Everyone knew the nuns adored the prissy little girl. And we all knew Janie took advantage of it.

We followed the two along the sidewalk in front of the school and paused to wait for the rest of the class to catch up. Once the line was assembled to Sister's satisfaction we continued to church. Just inside the front entrance, I dipped my fingertips into the small brass bowl that hung on the wall next to the door. The holy water clung to my fingers and moistened my forehead and shoulders as I made the sign of the cross. In the name of the Father, and of the Son and of the Holy Ghost, Amen, I whispered to myself. I still wondered about the Holy Ghost. The only ghost I knew was Casper. My thoughts were interrupted when the boys behind me began to shove each other as they reached for the holy water.

"A lil dab will do ya!" Steven said in a voice that was much too loud for church. The boys' laughter echoed in the nearly empty alcove. An elderly woman, shrouded in a long black mantilla, was kneeling in the last pew. She turned slightly and peeked around the edge of the lacy covering at the boys, quelling their antics.

As we began our procession down the middle aisle I heard an occasional creak from the old wooden pews. To some it would be creepy, but for me it was not. I felt comfort in the church.

The only light came from the propped open door at the front and several lit votive candles located near the altar. Cream colored stone pillars rose majestically from floor to ceiling every ten pews or so along the side aisles of the church. Bronze plaques that represented the Stations of the Cross, indicating the story of Jesus' crucifixion, hung on each of the round pillars. Narrow stained glass windows were built into the stone walls of the church. Details in the windows depicted angels and saints that I didn't know. A narrow flap hinged at the bottom of each window was propped open, letting in fresh air but no sunlight.

As we proceeded down the middle aisle I gazed above my head. Brilliant colors of light blue, white and gold adorned the domed ceiling. The colors represented the sky and clouds while the gold outlined many angels and trumpets. It was like peering through the gates of heaven.

"Walk very slowly, take your time," Sister whispered to each of us. "You are not in a race."

I looked down at the dark stone floor and slowed my pace, while my partner, Steven, continued on his way. He was a foot or so in front of me absentmindedly strolling with his hands in his pockets. Sister caught sight and immediately went to correct him. She pinched the shoulder of his shirt and gave it a tug, causing a tear in the fabric. The movement forced him back next to me but she made no apologies for what she had done. She got her point across.

Our group stopped for a moment while Sister Cornelius hurried to the front to decide where she wanted us to sit. I looked ahead at the sanctuary before me. A black wrought iron rail lined the front of the altar. Running along the length of it was a kneeler covered with red vinyl. It was there that people knelt in front of the priest to receive their host. And it was there that I would be making my First Holy Communion. Thinking about it caused a flutter of excitement in my stomach.

Beyond the railing was the most important place of all in the church. Wide polished marble steps led up to the altar. An enormous rectangle stone table was situated directly in the center. It was covered with a white lace cloth with the letter P and a gold x embroidered across the front of it.

Behind the table were six closets extending from floor to ceiling. The door panels were covered in gold filigree, each with a design of a simple cross, a lamb or a chalice. I wondered if the priest stored his vestments there or perhaps they lead to a secret passage. It was very mysterious.

Centered in the middle of the gold closets was the tabernacle that rested on its own marble table. The dome shaped structure was about two feet tall and looked like a miniature doll house. It was completely covered in gold except for a tiny white curtain in the front. I knew from attending church that the chalice and other special items used at Mass were put there.

Each week as we stayed in the kneeling position Father tidied up the altar table after communion. I watched as the altar boy added water to the chalice. Then the priest drank from it, wiped the glass and placed what looked like a white napkin and envelope on top. I wondered what could be inside the square white packet. Then he glided slowly over to the tabernacle and placed the items inside. When he was finished he sat on the giant red velvet chair located just to the left of the gold closets. We were finally allowed to sit down. As we waited silently, Father sat with his eyes closed in prayer. When he rose from his chair it signaled the end of Mass.

I gazed up, high above the tabernacle, to look at the gigantic crucifix. The artwork was amazing; Christ was so life-like with the crown of thorns and His sweat of blood. The many wounds on His battered body were so detailed it made me sad to look into His distraught face. His presence dominated the entire area.

I felt a nudge.

Steven pushed my arm. "Quit your gawking, Mulldoon! And sit down."

I quickly moved along the pew and took my seat. The way Sister had placed us I sat in the second pew directly in front of the candle display. The votive candles were provided for parishioners to light in reverence for their deceased loved ones or perhaps a special request. Every now and then, after mass, my grandmother gave me a nickel or dime to deposit into the tin cup next to the display. Then with her guidance I took the long wax taper and lit one end with the flame from a candle and then lit another in one of the rows. I said a silent prayer, sometimes for myself, sometimes for my family, sometimes for no reason at all.

"Listen and pay attention!"

Sister Cornelius snapped her fingers and waved her hand as she whispered loudly to get her class under control. She proceeded to demonstrate how we were to approach the communion rail.

"Hands are to remain folded in prayer as you kneel at the railing."

She knelt and turned to face us.

"Then wait for Father Murphy and the altar server to come to you."

Sister returned to her students and selected, who else, but Janie to demonstrate. Janie took her position on the red vinyl kneeler. The nun opened a small gate in the rail and stood on the opposite side, as the priest did each Sunday.

Steven was restless. The boy swung his legs wildly and he made bubbles with his spit as we watched the demonstration.

"Steven! Stop it!"

I knew if Sister Cornelius caught sight of him there would be hell to pay.

"Father will approach each of you with communion. He will say, 'This is the Body of Christ'."

She demonstrated to Janie.

"Your response will be 'Amen'. I want you to say it loud enough for Father to hear. Do not mumble. And just as he begins to give you the consecrated host, hold your tongue out slightly. The altar server will be right beside him holding the brass plate under your chin."

Janie opened her mouth and stuck out her tongue as Sister Cornelius pretended to give her communion.

"Once you have received the host, make the sign of the cross and bow your head. This is when you say a prayer thanking Jesus for communion."

Steven gave my arm a rough nudge causing me to look over at him. He was intentionally sticking his tongue out as far as he could but when Sister turned to us he immediately put it back in his mouth.

The nun gave one last very important instruction.

"Children, I must emphasize to you. Under no circumstances are you to chew or bite down on the host."

She paused, letting us absorb her words.

"Doing so will make the angels cry. Just let it melt in your mouth."

She leaned in and gave us a stern look.

"Again, remember, whatever you do, do not chew it. I will see you. Your parents will see you. But most importantly the angels will see you."

I swallowed hard. That was the last thing I wanted to do. It was something else for me to worry about. What if I absentmindedly began to chomp on the host?

"Does everyone understand?"

"Yes Sisterrrr" we said in unison.

"We can't eat it? What the hell?" Steven whispered in my ear. "Jesus Christ, they'd better taste good. I hope they taste like chocolate!"

I shoved my elbow into his arm. But his comment made me wonder. What *did* the host taste like?

Sister continued to show us how to leave the communion rail and proceed, single file up the marble steps of the altar where we would get a blessing from Father. At the top, right in front of his chair, the priest would pray over each one of us by placing his hand on top of our heads. After receiving his blessing we were instructed to turn and continue down the opposite side of the altar back to our seats.

It seemed easy enough.

First Holy Communion was 8:30 a.m. on Sunday, May 2, 1965. The day was warm and sunny, a perfect day for the joyous occasion.

I awoke early that morning excited and a little nervous for this important day in my life. My stomach rumbled with hunger but I knew the rules. We were not allowed to eat anything before church, especially if receiving communion. My mother helped me into my new white communion dress that Grammy Fitzpatrick bought for me weeks before. It was a chiffon dress with short sleeves trimmed in satin and a white silk ribbon that tied around my waist. I wore white ankle socks with lace around the edge and a brand new pair of shiny white patent leather shoes that made a nice clicking sound on the pavement. My mother fastened a thin crown of white silk flowers and pearls to the top of my head. It had a short white tulle veil that hung from the crown and it made me feel like a bride. The night before, my mother had put several pink sponge curlers in my hair as an attempt to straighten it. That morning she brushed them out and they looked perfect with the veil. When Grammy and Grampa Fitzpatrick arrived that morning, they gave me a First Communion gift. It was a white leather pouch containing a delicate strand of pink crystal rosary beads. The beads were beautiful but I thought it strange that on the inside of the pouch were typed instructions: In case of emergency please contact the nearest priest. Did that mean if something happened to me my parents would not be contacted first?

The 1965 First Communion class of St. Timothy's waited patiently in the school gymnasium. Sister Bridgette, the vice-principal was on hand to assist Sister Cornelius. Sister Bridgette was a mean looking nun who always appeared as though she was sucking on a lemon. Most of us called her Bugsy because her oversized yellowed teeth were similar to Bugs Bunny. The surly nun slowly paced back and forth across the gym reminding each of us to keep our hands folded in prayer and walk evenly with our partner.

"There is to be no rushing. Just walk slowly and reverently."

When anyone began to chat or squirm from being impatient Sister Bridgette was there in a flash.

"Mr. O'Hara!! Puhleeeeeze stand still."

Minutes later, as she busied herself with another student, Steven threw caution to the wind when he put his thumb on his nose and wriggled his fingers, showing everyone what he thought of Sister Bridgette.

The procession made it over to the church in perfect formation. Parents and relatives were already seated as space had been reserved for them near the front.

Everything went exactly as we had practiced. Surprisingly, we walked at the perfect pace and sat in the designated pews. Sister Cornelius never smiled but her demeanor told us she was pleased as she sat behind the last row of her students.

The mass was long, as usual, with a long-winded homily devoted to the new First Communion students. Father Murphy loved to hear himself talk. He droned on and on so much that I don't remember what he said, I was too excited to get my first host.

Finally, Father nodded to Sister Cornelius signaling us to proceed to the communion rail. Sister stood at the first row to be sure we followed her previous instructions.

The organist played *Holy, Holy, Holy* as I knelt down at the railing. The cushioned vinyl was much better than the hard floors at school but to be this close to the altar was a bit nerve wracking. It was very up close and personal to where

Father did all of his mysterious business. Even Steven was solemn and behaved himself. I felt my heart racing as I waited my turn. Out of the corner of my eye I could see Father Murphy and an altar boy slowly approaching. I recognized the eighth grade boy from school. I wasn't sure if I should look up at them or not so I stole a quick glance next to me as Eva MacDonald received her communion. Her tongue barely left her mouth. Father pinched the small tan wafer between his thick fingers and gently laid it on her tongue. The altar boy remained solemn as he held the brass plate under Eva's chin. She made the sign of the cross then bowed her head. I took a deep breath and waited my turn.

"This is the body of Christ."

I looked up at Father Murphy. His large hairy hand held the host right in front of my eyes.

"Amen."

I let my tongue out just a bit. Father reached and set the host in my mouth. I lowered my eyes and saw the brass plate under my chin. As Father and the altar boy moved to Steven, I blessed myself, bowed my head and closed my eyes.

But I didn't say any prayers. All I could think of was how it felt. The dry wafer immediately clung to the roof of my mouth. My tongue touched it several times before I remembered what Sister had said. After several minutes, while waiting for the others to receive, the host fell and began to dissolve on my tongue.

I relaxed. I didn't make the angels cry.

The host was like nothing I'd ever tasted before. It was not like any bread I'd ever eaten, but more like a stale cracker or a very bland unsweetened biscuit.

Thankfully, Steven received communion without incident. It took several minutes for Father Murphy to finish distributing hosts to the class and we knelt patiently as we listened to the organist play the familiar hymn over and over again.

Sister Cornelius remained next to Janie and waited for the priest. Father finished cleaning up the table on the altar then sat in his big red chair. With Sister's nod, Janie began the procession to receive the final blessing. We treaded very slowly, making our way up the polished marble steps. One by one, students paused in front of him. With his hand resting softly on my head Father prayed over me in Latin. I stared at the gold cross hanging from his neck as I inhaled the scent of his strong aftershave. When he removed his hand, I knew I was supposed to step away but suddenly my mind went blank. I forgot what I was supposed to do. I turned completely around and came face to face with Steven.

He rolled his eyes and whispered through clenched teeth, "Move Maureen! You're holding up the line."

Flustered, I felt my cheeks grow hotter by the second as I stood there trying to remember what to do. Steven gruffly brushed by me and stepped in front of Father. There I stood, alone, looking out to the sea of faces staring back at me. I spotted an exasperated Sister Cornelius who was gesturing to me to turn around and return to the opposite side of the altar. By now two more students had already been blessed and were returning to their seats. For some unknown reason I returned the same way I had gone up the altar. It was causing a ruckus as the remaining line of students had to shift and move aside to let me through but I didn't care. As I passed Sister Cornelius I avoided her disgusted look. Just as I returned to the pew, I met up with Steven.

"Way to mess up the line, Mulldoon! You're such a goddamned goon."

Tears welled up as I ignored his taunting and said nothing in fear that I would burst out crying. Mass finally came to an end and we processed out of church.

Sister Cornelius paused and nodded solemnly to my parents as my family greeted me outside. I was relieved that she continued on without saying a word about my mistake.

My parents took pictures of me as I stood proudly on the front steps of the church. Even though things had not gone as planned on the altar, I felt all grown up at the tender age of seven; knowing from that day forward I was allowed to participate in and receive Holy Communion every Sunday.

And although I didn't like the taste or the fact that I couldn't chew it, I knew in my heart that receiving that blessed host each week was one more way to get me into heaven.

1964 SOUTH PAW

Second grade was turning out to be quite a busy year at school. Along with preparing for two very important sacraments it was the year the nuns began to make demands on us. They no longer treated us like little children, even though we were. Expectations were high and they no longer tolerated any babyish behavior. It was a turning point for many of us.

One of those demands on the second graders was to discontinue printing and begin cursive writing. Penmanship was serious business at St. Timothy's and to enforce this, the nuns used any means of discipline.

Every afternoon during penmanship class Sister's voice echoed in my head as she commanded that our writing be legible and neat. We were taught the Palmer Method, a handwriting system that required all students to use their right hand.

There were no exceptions.

It was an unfortunate rule, especially for those naturally blessed with left handedness. For if so, he or she was quickly put in their place. I was grateful that I was not.

"It's the work of Satan!" Sister Mary Cornelius dramatically announced as she sauntered up and down the aisles throughout our lesson.

Every day we practiced by writing the letters of the alphabet across yellowed lined sheets of paper.

Day after day, week after week I watched the only two lefties in my class struggle with their assignments. Sister Cornelius used any tactic she deemed fit to accomplish the transformation she desired.

Seven-year-old Eva McDonald could write beautifully—with her left hand. Many times during art class I watched as she drew pretty pictures then signed and titled her art work, all with her left hand. Eva confided to me that her mother had her practicing writing at home every night. The discouraged girl said it was as complicated as trying to write with her foot; it just didn't feel natural. Unfortunately for Eva, none of the extra work was helping and she was not meeting Sister Cornelius' requirements. The nun was visibly frustrated and each week I could see the already shy Eva becoming more and more ashamed and withdrawn. I liked the quiet girl and I felt bad that she was in such a difficult position. Day after day it was increasingly uncomfortable to watch Eva and Shawn, the other leftie endure the repercussions.

Shawn Holland struggled more than Eva, although he didn't get as rattled when Sister Cornelius hovered over his desk.

One afternoon during penmanship Shawn's father came to the classroom to meet with Sister. She stood in the doorway with her back to us as she spoke to the man. The entire time she held one arm outstretched as she shook a finger at our class. No one dared to move. Without speaking a word or even looking at us she had control.

The man sadly dropped his head to his chest and mumbled, "Do what you have to do, Sister."

That was all she needed. His one statement opened the proverbial door for Sister Cornelius.

It started with threats.

Desperate to get her students to conform, Sister took out her ruler and slapped it softly into her palm as she strolled up and down the aisle often pausing next to Shawn. Periodically the loud crack of the wooden instrument against his desk made me jump. I turned around to see the boy's lips pursed in anger as he struggled to write on the lined paper.

"Next time this will be on that left hand of yours!" Sister threatened.

"Yes Sister."

Shawn's jaw was tightly clenched and as soon as the nun continued to the front of the room he stuck his tongue out in anger. With each passing day it became obvious that Eva was more and more nervous as Sister Cornelius paced up and down the aisles, the ruler clenched in her hand.

"Being left handed is the work of the devil! That's why you must, must learn the proper way to write!"

One afternoon I looked up to see Sister at Eva's desk observing the timid girl, who was slumped over as she concentrated to complete the required assignment. Her left hand was contorted like a tiny curled shrimp as it held her paper firmly in place. She bit the tip of her tongue as her right hand slowly moved the pencil. Eva's left hand writhed uncontrollably on top of the desk as she struggled to duplicate the sentence Sister had written on the blackboard. Eva was visibly shaking but remained intently focused on the sheet of paper.

"Now Eva, you must complete the letter before lifting the pencil off the paper. And please, please! Relax that left hand of yours!"

Sister's voice was quivering. The frustrated nun leaned over and rested her hand on Eva's desk. I stared at the bulging knuckles on her gruesome index finger. A long yellowed fingernail pointed to the girl's work. As Eva pressed the pencil further onto the paper the tip of the pencil snapped off. Eva looked up at Sister with a pained expression. My heart broke for her.

"Don't look at me like that, Miss McDonald! Just get up and go sharpen your pencil!"

Exasperated, Sister made her way to her next victim. Shawn was biting his lower lip as he wrote. The angry nun leaned in close to observe him.

Releasing a loud sigh she abruptly went to the blackboard. After drawing a small circle at the height of her chest she brushed her hands together to remove the excess chalk then called Shawn to the front.

"Perhaps you need to learn concentration, young man. Somehow, someway, I will get you to write the Palmer way!"

She maneuvered the boy in front of the blackboard and instructed him to stand on his toes. Then she had him place the end of his nose inside the circle. Shawn struggled to stay on the tips of his worn out shoes while keeping his nose against the board. The punishment was humiliating and difficult to watch. Sister Cornelius sat at her desk and observed Shawn from time to time as he struggled to stay in the position for the remainder of penmanship class.

By spring neither student had shown much improvement.

One afternoon Sister Cornelius sat at her desk, glaring at her two lefties. Her eyes squinted as she wrung her hands together. It was obvious she was contemplating something sinister and by the look on the nun's face I knew it couldn't be good. Her voice, deep and stern, let us know as well.

"Eva and Shawn come to the front."

Eva timidly made her way to Sister's desk as she clenched and unclenched her right hand which appeared cramped from all the writing. Shawn flippantly tossed his pencil onto his desk and sauntered to the nun's desk.

"This has gone on long enough. I have shown both of you over and over again how to write correctly."

That's when she reached into her drawer and grabbed her weapon.

"Miss MacDonald, hold out your hands."

Eva tentatively held her petite trembling hands out in front of her. Sister towered over her as she grabbed each of the girl's palms, twisting and flipping them towards the ceiling. Before Eva had time to brace herself, Sister smacked her palms with the wooden ruler.

"Left hand writing is the work of SATAN!" Sister Cornelius shouted. "Remove the devil's work and just do what I ask you to do!!"

My eyes grew wide and I swallowed the lump in my throat. The nun's eyes were glassy and red. Her thick black eyebrows were scrunched together casting an evil look.

She looked like the devil herself.

Eva began to cry softly but that didn't seem to faze Sister who continued to glare down at her prey. Eva turned away from the nun's intimidating stare. Her palms instantly turned red.

She managed a faint whisper.

"Y-y-es Sister."

"Now miss. Do you think you can go back and write properly? The way I taught you?"

"Y-y-y-yes Sister" Eva stammered.

"Good. Go back to your seat and prove it to me."

Eva quickly returned to her desk, sniffling and rubbing her hands together. It was obvious she was not only embarrassed, she was angry. Back in her seat, Eva grabbed her pencil and began to write. She fought back tears as she pressed the pencil hard onto the practice sheet.

"Mr. Holland, the devil has really gotten a hold of you!"

She snatched Shawn's grubby hands and quickly turned them over.

WHACK!

He barely flinched. Sister held the ruler high above her head, threatening Shawn once more.

But he never moved a muscle or said a word. His defiance seemed to have an effect on the nun because she dropped the ruler on her desk and sat down. Shawn's face was expressionless as he returned to his seat.

He'd won.

"The rest of you continue with your work. Or there will be more sore hands."

I lowered my head to avoid Sister's glare.

Within a week Eva's writing had shown a vast improvement. So much so, that Sister called upon her for a special assignment.

"Eva! Shawn! Come to the front please."

Oh, no, I thought. Here we go again.

"Please go to the blackboard," she said to the pair.

"Eva, you've done well and proved to me that you can now write the Palmer way."

She grabbed a piece of chalk and handed it to the girl.

"I want you to teach Shawn. For the love of God, show this boy what you've learned so that he can correct his penmanship."

Shawn was not giving up without a fight.

"Sister! That's not fair! I know how to write," he shouted. "I don't need a girl to teach me."

Sister Cornelius twisted his ear as she spoke to him very slowly.

"Mr. Holland, you'd...better...watch...your...tongue, young man! I am at my wits end with you!"

Shawn tried to step away but Sister had a tight grip on the edge of his ear.

"Eva has made tremendous progress. Perhaps she can help you. Lord knows you need all the help you can get!"

When she let go of his ear it was beet red.

"When I am satisfied with your progress, Mr. Holland, then you may go to recess."

Eva folded her arms in protest and looked at Shawn with disgust. It wasn't fair that play time depended on him, but there would be no use arguing.

"Eva, please write two sentences on the board and remember your grammar. Shawn, I want you to copy them precisely. I'm going to Sister Xavier's office for a moment so I'll check your progress when I return."

With that, she waddled out the door leaving our class alone. Everyone was silent as we watched the two at the blackboard. Eva was furious.

"Thanks a bunch, Shawn!"

"It's not my fault, Eva. Sister's making me do this. Just hurry up and write something so we can go outside."

"Write 'Sister's an old crow'!" shouted Steven. "Or hail to the penguin!"

"You'd better not!" Janie warned with her nose poised in the air.

Eva smiled mischievously at Steven. After a moment the brave girl began to write as Shawn stood next to her and read the sentences.

I couldn't believe what shy little Eva had done.

The boy giggled as he struggled to duplicate Eva's sentences. Once finished, the two stepped back and observed their work. The two laughed so hard that Eva had tears running down her cheeks.

"You're cool, Eva! Even I would never dare write that" Steven announced.

Others began to whisper and laugh.

"I'm telling Sister!" shouted Janie.

"I was just joking. Let's change it before Sister comes back"

Eva grabbed an eraser.

"Hurry up!"

But it was too late.

The labored breathing and the sound of her legs rubbing together let everyone know Sister had returned before we actually saw her. She stopped abruptly in the doorway. With her hands on her hips, chest heaving to catch her breath, she stared at the blackboard.

We are not Satan.

Sister Corn is.

Our class was quickly dismissed for recess, but not before we heard the two sharp smacks of Sister's ruler. When we returned from the playground Eva and Shawn were busy at the blackboard. Occasionally Shawn rubbed his hands together. Eva was sniffling, her face flushed. She was almost finished her new assignment.

The new sentence on the board said it all.

I am sorry for all my sins. Sister is not the devil.

Eva and Shawn eventually met Sister Cornelius' requirements and in June the two Southpaws were promoted to third grade.

The problem children now belonged to Sister Mary Oliver.

1965 BUBBLER AND BAZOOKA

I t was an early Thursday morning; the Feast of the Ascension, and our third grade class was preparing to attend the required mass to celebrate the Holy Day of Obligation. Our teacher, Sister Oliver, instructed us to line up single file along the freshly polished mahogany walls out in the hall. Lemon polish and a fresh coat of floor cleaner permeated the corridor.

As luck would have it, I ended up standing directly behind Steven. We waited as patiently, as any eight year olds could while the nuns scurried about making sure everyone was accounted for and prepared to go, as the classes would be walking over to church together. The nuns liked to impress the locals by parading their protégés to mass.

It wasn't long before some of the students became restless. Patrick O'Sullivan, who was in front of Steven, ran his finger along the gleaming mahogany wall drawing imaginary pictures. The normally well-behaved boy was quite fidgety as he twisted his head back and forth as he looked up and down the hall. Patrick couldn't be still for a second. Suddenly he began to cough incessantly.

It sounded fake, as though forced so the constant noise was becoming extremely irritating to those around him.

"Jesus, O'Sullivan, go get a drink!" sneered Steven as he gave Patrick a shove. Obviously I wasn't the only one that was annoyed.

Without hesitation the hyper boy sprinted across the hall to the water bubbler, breaking an all important rule. He was taking his chances as Sister had instructed us to stay in our designated spot. If we were caught leaving without permission it would surely result in punishment.

I searched the area for Sister and breathed a sigh of relief to discover her at the opposite end of the hall, chatting with Principal Xavier. Luckily for Patrick she wasn't paying attention to what was happening at our end of the corridor. For what seemed like an eternity, Patrick gulped the water that spurted from the white porcelain fountain. He slurped continuously never coming up for air.

Everyone watched in horror.

"That dink's gonna be peeing in the pew if he keeps it up!"

"Look at him for Christ's sake!"

"Patrick is just asking for trouble!"

I shook my head as I watched. If Patrick continued at that rate he'd definitely end up with a wicked stomach ache and a very full bladder.

Before anyone could stop him Steven ran across the hall to the bubbler.

"Steven!" I whispered aloud. That boy was either very courageous or very dumb.

Sister Mary Oliver and Sister Xavier were nowhere in sight. And thankfully, the other nuns were still in their classrooms. I grew anxious; wishing that the boys would just return to the line.

Kids around me began to whisper desperately across the hall.

"Hey! Get back!"

"You're gonna get us all in big trouble!"

"Come on! Sister will be back any minute!"

Students pleaded with them to hurry back before they were caught in the act. But the boys did not heed the warnings. Patrick glanced up at Steven out of the corner of his eye, as he finally stopped drinking and snarled at the boy.

"Wait your turn, O'Hara."

"Jesus, O'Sullivan, don't ya think ya had enough water ya little shit? Ya gonna be pissing your pants in church!"

Patrick ignored the remarks and turned back to the stream of water. Steven leaned in closer to him. And his smirk told me that he was up to no good.

Don't do it, I thought to myself.

"Hey, got a piece of paper or somethin'?"

Patrick stood erect and finally stopped drinking as he wiped his mouth with his sleeve.

"What are you thinking?"

"Just answer me. Do ya or don't ya?"

Steven held out his hand, coaxing his partner in crime.

He wasn't quite a bully, but Steven had a way of convincing others to join in his shenanigans. I leaned against the wall and wondered what prank he was concocting this time.

Patrick searched his pockets and found a piece of Bazooka chewing gum.

"Oh yeah, that'll work! Hand it over!"

Steven grabbed the piece of gum and unwrapped it. He popped the hard sugary square into his mouth and chewed it for a few seconds to soften it. Then he wadded it up with his fingers and crammed the pink sticky glob into one of the holes of the spout. Everyone recognized the gum and began whispering.

"Steven's chewing gum!"

"Patrick has gum at school!"

The nuns made it perfectly clear that gum was strictly forbidden.

"Beat it!!" Steven called out as the two boys ran across the hall and quickly stepped back into line.

"Let's see who the next sucker is to get it in the eye!"

Steven wore a sly smile as he tried to look innocent with his thumbs in his pockets. It didn't take long to find out. Within minutes their unsuspecting victim sauntered up to the bubbler and bent down to get a drink.

My stomach did a flip flop.

Sister Mary Oliver firmly held her large white collar against her chest and leaned over the bubbler. I could feel my heart pounding. Somehow this felt wrong. But Steven and Patrick didn't seem fazed at all as they exchanged glances and smiles.

"This is going to be sooooo good!" Steven whispered with a slow nod.

Everyone watched as Sister pursed her lips and put her face deep into the small basin. She extended her right hand from the long black sleeve and pressed the button on the side to release the water. I glanced over at the boys who were grinning from ear to ear showing no concern whatsoever. It amazed me. No one in their right mind would ever mess with the water fountain.

"AAAAHHHH!"

Her loud outburst startled me as a stream of cold water shot up in a perfect vertical line hitting Sister Oliver directly in the face. As if in slow motion, the water saturated the nun's headpiece and veil and splattered across the lenses of her silver cats' eye glasses. She spun around to face us as she desperately wiped the water that was streaming down her cheeks. I gulped when I saw how angry she was.

"WHO...DID...THIS??"

Sister Oliver stepped slowly across the hall as she continued to dry her face with her billowy sleeve. Drops of water clung to the edge of her wimple and veil. Before I knew it she was directly in front of me. I could barely see her angry eyes through the smeared moisture on her glasses. Water droplets rolled down her lenses and fell to her heaving chest while large damp stains began creeping across her white collar. Not wanting to make eye contact I looked down at the floor after stealing a glance at the two boys. Patrick's eyes were as wide as saucers and his jaw hung toward the floor. Unfazed, Steven stifled a laugh as he looked at the water soaked nun. He was, however, the only one laughing.

I was scared stiff and could feel my heart thumping in my chest.

"WHO ON EARTH DID THIS??"

Sister Oliver removed her glasses and cleaned them off with the sleeve of her habit but without her thick lenses she couldn't see a thing in front of her. Her eyes were squinted as she leaned in for a closer look and stared directly into Patrick's face. Her soaked bushy eyebrows began drooping.

"WHO IS RESPONSIBLE FOR THIS? Someone had better tell the TRUTH!"

The entire class remained quiet until we heard that all too familiar squeaky voice.

"I know who did it, Sister."

Janie proudly raised her hand. Steven looked behind me, pursed his lips and shot the tattletale a threatening look. I too turned to Janie and mouthed NO pleading the girl to remain quiet. There was the slight chance Sister might never find out.

But the bratty girl kept talking; the teacher's pet couldn't keep her trap shut. Janie managed to take the fun out of everything. She knew the nuns adored her so she wasn't afraid of Steven, or anyone else for that matter, and was able to ignore all the nasty looks.

Sister's voice and demeanor quickly changed.

"Janie, dear, did you see who was at the bubbler?"

The nuns always took her side.

"Yeessss, Sister. It was Steven and Patrick" Janie sang like a bird, as she twisted her body back and forth and pointed a bony finger at the two boys. I followed her gesture to Patrick. The poor kid looked like he'd just seen a ghost. He gulped and absentmindedly rubbed his belly. Steven, however, looked extremely calm, as he stood quietly with his thumbs tucked into his front pockets. Sister planted her feet firmly in front of the two spirited boys.

"Steven and Patrick, did you do something to the bubbler?"

Sister Oliver was a domineering presence as she stood with her hands firmly on her hips. Steven couldn't help himself. When he looked up at the nun he stifled one chuckle, then another as he watched several drops of water cling precariously from her glasses. As she spoke the droplets swayed back and forth. He shrugged his shoulders and looked down at his feet trying to compose himself.

"Tell the TRUTH, Steven! For once in your life tell the blessed truth!!"

It would be worse if he lied.

"THE TRUTH!"

The nun left him no choice.

"We were thirsty, Sister. We just got a drink!" Steven blurted out.

"So you got out of line, did you? Come with me, Mr. O'Hara"

Sister Oliver grabbed his upper arm and dragged him over to the bubbler.

"Is this your gum stuck in here?"

Sister pointed to the pink wet wad crammed into the spout. Steven leaned over and looked into the basin.

"Nope, that's not my gum."

Steven emphatically shook his head.

"So you're telling me, Mr. O'Hara, that you did not bring gum to school?"

Her voice was now a few octaves higher. Steven continued his denial.

"If it's not your gum, then do you know how it got there, Mr. O'Hara?"

Sister pinched his upper arm even harder as he tried to pull away.

"Okay, okay!! I put it there! But it's not my gum, Sister!"

It was no time to be a smart ass. Sister Oliver was obviously running out of patience. She let go of his arm and yanked the edge of Steven's ear, twisting it as she began to question through the clenched teeth.

"Mr. O'Hara! I have had it with you! Our Lord in heaven is watching you! Now, you'd better tell the truth, once and for all!"

Steven's distorted ear, as well as his cheeks, began to turn bright red. He was trying to turn his head away but it only made things worse. Ultimately, he turned in his accomplice.

"Okay, okay Sister! I got the gum from Patrick!" Steven winced. "Ow!"

I swallowed hard as I watched the fuming nun let go of his ear and turn quickly on her heel.

Sister Oliver stormed back across the hall and approached Patrick. It was at that moment Patrick peed his pants, right there in front of God and all of us. The visible stream saturated the front of his khaki pants, continued down his pant leg and spilled onto the gleaming hardwood floor. I covered my mouth with both hands and watched in horror as Patrick's pants became soaked. His eyes filled with tears and his bottom lip began to quiver as he looked up at Sister. My heart ached for Patrick O'Sullivan.

"Mr. O'Sullivan, is that true? Do you have chewing gum?"

The color drained from Patrick's face.

"You know that it is against school rules, do you not, Mr. O'Sullivan?!"

Sister Oliver leaned in and came face to face with Patrick. She was completely unaware that he was still urinating right in front of her. A puddle was forming around his brown leather shoes and as usual his laces were not tied and were soaking in the smelly mess. Patrick couldn't answer. He'd never been in this kind of trouble before.

"Patrick, I am talking to you!! Did...you...give.... Steven...a ...piece...of...gum?"

She asked through clenched teeth.

"I—I—I…" Patrick began to stutter.

Frustrated, Sister Oliver reached out and grabbed his right ear. Clenching it she led him across the hall and placed him next to Steven.

"You boys have a lesson to learn! Now come with me."

As she yanked an ear from each boy Sister pulled them into the nearest classroom, oblivious of the trail of pee that trailed behind. The putrid smell of urine was becoming stronger. I couldn't believe Sister didn't notice the puddle that had formed right in the corridor. She had to have walked right through it.

"EEEWW!" exclaimed several students as they held their noses.

I watched Sister Oliver drag the boys away while some of the kids began pointing and covering their noses.

"That is disgusting!" exclaimed Janie as she dramatically held her nose.

"Shut up, you ratfink! It's because of you they're in trouble!"

Francis O'Neal, the tallest boy in class, got out of line and confronted Janie.

"You shoulda kept your big prissy mouth shut!"

He was threatening as he towered over her pointing a finger at her face.

"I'm telling Sister!" Janie whined as she took a step back.

The students around Janie also stepped back, clearing the path for Francis, who wasn't letting up.

He stepped even closer to the girl and began to mimic her.

"I'm telling Sister! I'm telling Sister! McMack, you'd better watch out or I'll stick YOUR head in the bubbler! Then you'll get cooties!"

"EW!" several of the kids exclaimed. "Cootie shot! Cootie shot!"

Janie got the message loud and clear. She leaned back against the wall, crossed her arms, and looked straight ahead with her nose tilted in the air.

Feeling confident she'd remain quiet, Francis returned to his place in line.

I was relieved that someone had finally spoken up to Janie. After a minute or so I became curious as to what Sister was doing with the boys. Feeling brave, I carefully scanned the hall to be sure no other nuns were in sight then quickly tiptoed to peek inside the classroom, located just a few feet away.

Sister stood directly in front of the two boys, next to a desk in the first row and she looked angry. As she lifted the lid of the desk she placed the right hand of each boy on the inside edge.

The Hand Crunch!

I'd heard of the punishment but had never seen it happen. Steven looked so brave. But poor Patrick was shaking and crying softly. The nun did not waste any time. It all happened so quickly the boys didn't have a chance to brace themselves.

BAM!

I jumped as the heavy maple cover of the desk slammed firmly onto their hands.

"Ow!" Steven cried out as Patrick began to sob uncontrollably.

I squeezed my eyes shut for an instant and covered my mouth to keep from crying out. I could not believe they were being punished like this because of a little water.

"No gum is allowed in school! Do you hear me, you little hoodlums?"

She lifted the lid then smacked it down once more.

"And NO GUM IN THE BUBBLER!"

Sister's face appeared sinister and her cheeks were dark red. She lifted the desk cover and let them remove their hands.

"I hope you two learned your lesson!"

Both boys slowly rubbed their knuckles. Steven gave no indication of pain but when he looked over at Patrick and saw the front of the boy's pants he wrinkled his nose.

"Get back in line, boys. It's time for Mass."

Just as Sister turned on one heel I sprinted back to my place in line. My heart was racing. Sister Oliver stood at attention by the classroom door. If she noticed Patrick's pissy pants, she never said a word. The boys followed her out into the corridor. Patrick looked like he had a load in his drawers as he walked with his legs wide apart and shifted from side to side. I couldn't imagine she would allow him go to church like that.

Finally, Sister Xavier came out into the hall and rang the brass hand bell. The nuns led us over to church and everyone filed into the pews. Everyone in class was doing their best to avoid sitting next to stinky Patrick. I was glad to see Steven was sticking by his accomplice. The two boys sat side by side, directly in front of me. Poor Patrick, the unwilling partner in yet another of Steven's pranks, paid the ultimate price by sitting in wet stinky pants all day and with a throbbing hand too.

The altar server rang the bells signaling the start of Mass and the priest processed across the altar. I had to hold my breath when we stood as a pungent waft of urine made its way to my nose. Steven leaned over and nudged Patrick, who was still sniffling and wiping his face with his sleeve.

"Quit your cryin', O'Sullivan. It'll be alright."

He glanced around him before he said, "Next time we'll just kill the old bitch."

No one heard my gasp or the boys' hysterics for that matter for just at that moment the organist began to play *Holy God We Praise Thy Name* on the resounding pipe organ.

1966 SPRING CLEANING
FOR MARY

Believing cleanliness was next to Godliness, the Sisters of the Blessed Sacrament put us to work each spring scrubbing the school from top to bottom. In the month of May, as a way to honor the Blessed Virgin Mary, the nuns also prepared for the annual May Procession, a special mass where we praised the mother of God.

Windows were opened wide to let in the crisp, clean air as generous lilac bushes blooming right outside fragranced the classrooms. Each student was given a responsibility to carry out the cleaning assignments. Most duties were easy but there was one that I particularly avoided, and that was cleaning the life-sized religious statues. Intricately sculpted and hand painted with such exquisite detail, the explicit artwork made them appear very much alive. If I stared at them long enough I'd swear they were breathing. From the time I was in first grade I was haunted by the life sized replica of Jesus. God's eyes seemed to follow me whenever I passed Him. Other statues prominently displayed throughout the school gave me the same feeling. All were just as tall as the Jesus statue and located at opposite ends of the corridor, on both levels of the school. On the second floor a detailed replica of St Timothy welcomed his students as he gazed down the hall, arms outstretched. His painted face looked as though he would break out in a grin at any second.

Sister Mary Alexander, my fourth grade teacher, was handling spring cleaning duties in 1966.

Sister was younger than most, but not as young as Sister Claire, our music teacher. It was refreshing to see these two newcomers. Most days their faces brightened our day in comparison to the drab dreary look of the older nuns.

Always energetic, Sister Alexander was tall, lean and athletic. Every day she hustled and bustled around the classroom. Her long black veil blew out on the sides whenever she walked down the corridor, creating a wide canopy. She always looked as though she was on an urgent mission.

Lists were written on the blackboard with student's names and appointed cleaning assignments.

On Monday morning I began to scan the board for my name. I knew the nuns were extremely particular when selecting someone to clean the precious statues. They wanted a student who was not only responsible enough to work alone but who would take great care of the holy icons. Before I had a chance to finish, Sister Alexander called me to the front of the class.

I tentatively approached her desk.

I felt uneasy as Sister silently gave me the once over while pursing her lips.

"Maureen, since Janie is absent today you will take her place. I believe you're responsible enough to clean the statues."

I gulped nervously and responded by nodding my head. I had no choice.

"You may begin on the first floor."

Why couldn't I have gotten the fun job of polishing the floors like the boys did? Everyone knew that was the easiest thing to do. Those helpers were given a bundle of cloth rags and a can of lemon furniture polish. After tying a rag around each of their shoes they slowly skated up and down the hall as they sprayed the floor. I looked enviously at Steven and Francis who were already enjoying their "chore".

In my head I tried to rationalize Sister's decision. Perhaps she chose those particular boys because they were never out of her sight. At least I would be on my own as I wandered around the building, far away from Sister's hovering.

Sister Alexander handed me a wooden milk crate to use as step stool, a bucket full of warm soapy water that smelled like Lestoil and some old terry cloth towels. I flung the towels over my shoulder and made my way downstairs.

I stood outside the first grade classroom and looked up at Jesus. I had no choice but to face my fear. His face was extremely detailed; as were the bloodied wounds on the palms of His hands. I climbed the milk crate, took a deep breath and softly wiped the top of Jesus' head. My fingers stroked the realistic facial features and I paused to look into His eyes. I thought back to a time when I was in second grade. My class had just been taught the biblical account of one of the apostles, Doubting Thomas. After hearing that story I was never able to look at the statue the same way again. I wondered what would happen if I touched His hands. Would my fingers slip through those nail punctures? I continued and slowly wiped the sleeves but hesitated when I reached His palms. I repeated to myself, it's only a statue it's only a statue, nothing is going to happen. Still feeling apprehensive I held my breath and reached out hesitantly. I placed my index finger on the palm of His right hand and tentatively moved it towards the center, touching the painted blood. The next time I looked up into Jesus' face I immediately felt my breathing change and I was calmer. I could only imagine how Thomas must have felt!

I finished working my way down to His sandaled feet. Stepping back to observe my work, I was proud for overcoming a fear I'd carried inside of me. I bowed slightly, in reverence to Him then picked up my supplies and headed to the front of the school. I glanced into some of the classrooms and observed students scrubbing windows, wiping down blackboards and cleaning the tops of the desks. The smell of Windex was throughout the corridor. Everyone was busy but the nuns made sure chatter was kept to a minimum.

Lugging the cumbersome wooden crate, bucket and supplies I climbed the front stairs to a small landing. A tall statue of a Guardian Angel was centered in front of the enormous window facing Church Street. At night, the street light illuminated the angel's silhouette and it was an awesome sight to see. I carefully stepped onto the box and stretched to clean the androgynous face. Standing on tiptoe I took in the details of the carved facial features as I quickly wiped them clean.

Suddenly I heard the faint sound of someone crying. I stepped down from the box and went to the top of the stairs to listen. When I heard it again I left my cleaning supplies to follow the sobs. The sounds took me to one of the storerooms, just around the corner. The door was ajar and the room was dimly lit but I could see someone crouched low to the floor. I carefully pushed the door open.

It was Ellen. She was kneeling in front of a tabletop statue of St. Francis of Assisi. His outstretched hands were broken off.

"Hey, what's the matter? Are you okay?"

Ellen sniffed and wiped her yes with her sleeve. "Look!"

I followed Ellen's gesture and saw pieces of colored porcelain scattered on the floor.

"Oh geez! What happened?"

"I just looked away for a second and the whole thing fell to the floor!"

Ellen wiped her eyes with the back of her hands.

"So I picked up all the pieces I could find and moved it in here. Sister is going to kill me!"

"Okay, don't panic."

I had an idea. I quickly stood and quietly closed the door then turned on the lights.

"Let's look for some glue. There's got to be some here. We'll put it back together and no one will even notice!"

We began to pull out drawers and search a closet.

"Here! Let's try this!" Ellen called out after finding a bottle of Lepage's glue. "But we have to work fast."

I turned off all but one light so not to attract any attention then we sat on the floor and began to repair St. Francis. Ellen squeezed drops of the sticky, amber liquid onto each piece and together we began to salvage the saint. We had a limited amount of time, and we couldn't see that well, but after five minutes we stepped back and observed our work.

"Looks okay to me!" Ellen whispered.

I dumped the sticky bottle of glue into a drawer and peeked out into the hall.

"It's good enough. Come on let's put him back before anyone sees us."

Ellen hugged the statue as she sprinted to a marble table located in the stairwell. St. Francis of Assisi was put safely back into position. Ellen grabbed her cleaning supplies and rushed quickly back to the classroom.

"I have to hurry," she whispered. "Sister's probably wondering what happened to me. Thanks for helping!"

I lunged back up to the landing and gave the Guardian Angel a quick cleaning. I had to hurry as well, in case Sister Alexander came looking for me. By the end of the day the entire school smelled fresh and clean. The corridors' wood walls and floors gleamed from the incessant polishing. All of the windows, desks and blackboards were freshly washed and ready for this spring season. Sister Alexander was pleased with the results.

Four weeks passed....

Ellen and I thought it was a miracle and were certain that angel had been watching over us.

With puzzled looks, Sister Alexander and Sister Xavier carefully examined the statue. Something did not look right. Thick, brown glue oozed out between the uneven pieces and had dried into darkened congealed gobs.

Ellen and I glanced at one another and grinned, thankful that it had taken this long for anyone to notice.

Poor St. Francis now had lobster claws.

1967 RED ROVER, RED ROVER

Whether there were blustery winds, freezing temperatures or snow flurries, the nuns at St. Timothy's sent their students outside for at least 35 minutes each day. Used for recess, our playground was a paved parking lot located at the back of the school that was shared with the church. On days when there was a funeral or special mass, cars filled the lot creating a much smaller play area. There were no jungle gyms, swings, slides or any other play equipment so we became creative with our precious freedom outside of the classroom.

During each recess there was always one nun in charge. In addition to monitoring any rough play, that nun appointed two students to sell ice cream during the warmer months and miniature bags of chips during the fall and winter, as a way to raise money for the school. The boxes of frozen treats were donated by the local grocery store. More than once Ellen and I had been given the responsibility for sales. We were expected to sell all of the ice cream and I dreaded the task, as it interfered with play time. The job entailed standing at the side door of the school and waiting for those lucky students with money to purchase a Popsicle or ice cream sandwich. While one of us handed out the treats, the other collected the cash. I heard over and over again "will you share with me" from the unlucky ones who didn't have the means to buy. Something we were taught must have sunk in because sure enough kids complied as they used the corner of the brick building to split the treat in half to share with a classmate.

On the days I didn't have to sell ice cream or chips, I took part in any number of games. We formed teams to participate in the all-time favorite, TV tag. I was great at this game, perhaps because I watched too much television. Shows like The Munsters, The Flying Nun and Gilligan's Island were my favorites and I knew the characters and theme songs by heart. But even though I knew a lot of TV trivia I was rarely allowed to be 'it' or the leader. That position seemed to always go to Janie McMack.

Janie was the class pet so if anyone argued with her she went directly to the nun on duty and ultimately got her way. As the only spoiled child of an older couple she turned getting her way into an art. And the nuns absolutely adored her. They constantly doted on her and believed every word the whiny girl said. Many times after church, I overheard my parents discussing her family and the rumored substantial financial contributions they made to the parish.

Janie was a petite girl with long golden hair that had just the right amount of curl. I, as well as every other girl in class, was envious of Janie's beautiful locks. After all, my thick auburn waves were unruly at best unless my mother pulled them into two tight pigtails. Hard as I tried, my hair never looked like Janie's.

Even Sister Mary Bridgette voiced her opinion.

On a very chilly November afternoon several of us girls huddled together to gossip. Bugsy had playground duty that day and had been standing close by eavesdropping on our conversation about Janie. She sauntered over and forced her way into the group. Her face expressed disdain as she turned to me.

"You, my dear, should never, ever wear any shade of red with your hair color", she said with an insidious smile. "Red, pink, it will all clash with that atrocious hair of yours! Never mind those ruddy cheeks!"

Her brutal comment made me cringe. The nun seemed to enjoy ridiculing others.

"Yes Sister."

I never imagined her comment would sit on my mind for decades.

I was 10 and had no desire to fuss with my hair like some girls. I had more important things to do, like beating the boys at a game of marbles. Little Janie never considered getting on her belly and crawling on the gritty cold pavement to challenge the boys. But I did. As soon as the snow began to melt, a game of marbles took place in the school yard. Before long I became known as a pretty good competitor. So much so, that over the years I accumulated some nice aggies and cats eyes from the boys. And I accepted any challenge even if it meant laying on the ground, skirt and all, to get a good shot. I did whatever it took to win. Eventually Steven recognized me as a threat to his game which only encouraged him to practice more.

Janie, on the other hand, was too lady-like and prissy to participate, which only emphasized the contrast between her and the rest of us. She refused to join her classmates for a slide down the icy slope behind the church. Each winter students forged a safe path up a steep incline directly behind the church. Bundled up with layers upon layers of warm clothing we moved slowly due to the bulkiness. Snow pants, boots, parkas, mittens and hats covered us from head to toe. The incline created the perfect hill for sliding on ice. Always in the shade, the slope stayed ice-covered for months. Once we climbed the path and reached the top we stood directly behind a wide stained glass window. One by one we perched on the ledge for a second or two before sliding down the icy patch. Miraculously, that window stayed intact every year.

We never used toboggans or metal flying saucers, just the seat of our snow pants. Some of the daring ones, mostly the older boys, stood and slid on their boots. It was a quick, fun but potentially dangerous ride. Occasionally someone would fall and get hurt and that's when the nun in charge blew her whistle and immediately demanded everyone to stop. But the sliding always resumed the following day.

When Janie did decide to participate in games it was usually in a game called Red Rover.

"Red Rover, Red Rover, send Janie right over!"

Because of her delicate stature the girl was never able to break through the opposing human chain which caused frustration with the players. With each turn Janie ran back and forth trying her best but was ultimately captured by the opposing team.

One day I faced Janie as she prepared to come our way. Standing together with my teammates I helped form the solid chain. Francis, the team captain called out.

"Red Rover, Red Rover send Janie right over!"

Janie took several delicate steps backward. The other children on her team encouraged her to muster her strength and run as fast as she could. The girl took off running. Her arms flailed along her sides as she ran on the tips of her toes. I was surprised at her determination. Janie was running faster than I'd ever seen. Her face flushed deep red and her perfect golden curls bounced wildly. Suddenly she was right in front of me. At the last second Ellen and I tightened our grip but much to our surprise Janie broke through. Ellen and I looked at one another in shock then we began to laugh hysterically.

"Can you believe it! Prissy little Janie!!"

Then we heard the whistle.

Weeeet! Weeet! Weeeeeeeet!

A sharp shrill penetrated the air. We turned to see Sister Alexander running towards us as she blew the whistle excitedly. Her black habit and long veil billowed out as she ran. I looked around, wondering what had her so upset. I hadn't even noticed Janie, who was directly behind us, laying face down on the pavement.

Her plaid skirt was twisted up around her bottom exposing her navy blue tights and I could make out the faint print of her flowered underpants.

Sister Alexander knelt beside the girl and smoothed Janie's curls from her face. No one else attempted to help. Everyone watched silently as Sister turned Janie on to her side. Suddenly the girl burst out crying. Her pretty face turned ugly as she sobbed and dramatically reached out for Sister Alexander. Sister reassured her as she caressed the girl's back.

"There, there, dear! You'll be alright!"

Janie managed to sit up and looked directly at me and Ellen. Her nose was scuffed pink and she had tiny red scrapes on her freckled cheeks.

"You hateful little brats, you did that on purpose!" Janie screeched as she pointed to the two of us.

"You pushed me!"

My mouth dropped open. She couldn't be serious.

"You broke through the chain, Janie! That's part of the game." I shouted back.

"Don't be such a stupid cry baby!" Francis O'Neal called out to her.

"Yes, you did! You're a jerk, Maureen! You pushed me and you know it!"

The little witch was trying to blame me.

As Sister Alexander helped her to her feet I had to hold back my laughter. Janie McMack was quite a sight. Her once beautifully styled hair was tussled and tangled all over her head. Blotchy red scrapes from the pavement covered her face and her lower lip was swelling with every passing second. But the funniest thing was Janie's tights. As Sister adjusted the girl's skirt and wiped the tears from Janie's face with a tissue, no one could take their eyes off her legs. Janie's navy blue tights had two gaping holes in each knee and the contrast between her pale cream skin and dark stockings was hilarious. They looked like two large round eyes staring straight ahead. One by one, children began to giggle until everyone was laughing hysterically. Janie hadn't even noticed her tights yet. As Sister escorted her, the girl limped along, whimpering in pain. When she reached down to adjust her sagging stockings she discovered her knees protruding through the holes. She stopped and looked down at her legs. Her eyes grew wide in horror and she wailed like an injured animal. I'm sure she was mortified to be seen in such disarray.

Sister Alexander paused and glared directly at me.

"You, young lady!! Do you see what you've done?? I shall deal with you later!!" she said through clenched teeth.

"But Sister, it wasn't my fault. It's part of the game!"

"I am stopping this game. Go find something else to do!" bellowed Sister. "ALL OF YOU!"

I watched as Janie limped into school with Sister gently holding her arm. I didn't feel any pity for the girl, after all she knew the rules of the game.

Once Sister Alexander was far enough away Francis began his imitation of the nun. He squatted low to the ground, flapped his arms and paraded back and forth.

"No more games! You snotty little brats! You hurt Janie! Quack, quack, quack!"

Francis' voice went up several octaves as he waddled in a circle swinging imaginary rosary beads.

"Quack, quack, quack! Caw, caw, caw!"

Francis loved an audience and he surely had one that afternoon.

1967 RECESS IS FOR KIDS

Often times, older girls from the seventh grade invited me to play Double Dutch, mostly so they could be the ones to skip rope. But I didn't care. I knew one day when I proved myself by swinging the ropes evenly and steadily, they'd let me join in and skip while they sang one of the popular rhymes for me.

Mary Beth Finnegan was extremely good at Double Dutch. And because she brought the ropes to school each day, she was a bit bossy and always determined which rhyme would be said.

"Twenty four robbers!" she announced as she rocked back and forth on her heels just before heading in between the two criss-crossed ropes.

I sang loudly to Mary Beth as I swung the two long ropes in rhythmic motion with a seventh grader on the other end.

"Not last night, but the night before. Twenty four robbers came knockin' at my door".

Mary Beth jumped steadily for the entire verse then exclaimed, "Go faster!"

We twirled the ropes so fast they were a blur, until she eventually tripped and ended her turn.

"May I join you girls?"

I couldn't believe who was asking. It was Sister Claire. She was our music teacher and was very young pretty nun. She was also the only one from the Sisters of the Blessed Sacrament who seemed to truly care about her students. A day never went by that she wasn't wearing a huge smile. Although surprised by her request we were happy to swing the ropes for her.

"Yes, Sister!"

It was not a common occurrence to have a nun join in our activities and we glanced at one another as Sister Claire clenched bunches of her long black habit and raised the skirt up to her knees exposing shapely legs covered in black hose. It was the first time I had ever seen a nun's legs and I felt embarrassed to view them. Sister Claire counted, "One, two, three!" before jumping in between the twirling ropes. As her black veil bounced on her head a sudden gust of wind caught her veil and I caught a glimpse of long dark hair gathered in a small pony tail at the nape of her neck. My mouth dropped open.

The white starched wimple fit so tight around Sister's face and chin that it never moved an inch. Her smiling face beamed with delight. The large white collar covering her chest bounced up and down striking her chin but Sister Claire continued to jump and giggle with laughter. Her laugh was sweet and cheerful.

"Sing...a....song...for....me!" Sister Claire said haltingly as she continued to jump.

Mary Beth began the familiar rhyme and the rest of us joined her calling out "not last night but the night before". Sister Claire managed to jump throughout the whole rhyme before stopping. She stood between the ropes, hands on her hips.

"Phew! I haven't done that in years!" she exclaimed breathlessly.

A small crowd had gathered to watch and they applauded and cheered for Sister Claire.

Weeeet! Weeeeeet!!

Again the whistle.

Sister Alexander marched briskly across the playground towards us. She did not look happy. Her arms swung violently against the sides of her body. Her veil blew towards the rear as she walked directly to Sister Claire. Sister Alexander's lips were tightly wrapped around the whistle and her dark wiry eyebrows were pulled together meeting in the middle. Sensing trouble, I slowly began to back up. I had had enough of Sister Alexander's accusations for one day.

Still chuckling, Sister Claire never saw the angry nun heading her way.

"Sister Mary Claire! Sister Claire! You should be ashamed!!"

When Sister Claire spun around she found herself face to face with Sister Alexander and instantly began toying with her rosary beads.

"But Sister…."

"Recess is for our students, Sister!" Sister Alexander declared. "You are not a child."

She took Sister Claire by the elbow and turned her away from us.

"Now go back inside and prepare for your next class. We will discuss this later!"

Sister Claire looked sheepishly to the ground and softly said, "Yes, Sister."

She wiped her eyes as she quickly went back inside the school. Meanwhile, Sister Alexander never let me out of her sight for the rest of recess. I knew I had not done anything wrong. But somehow I was still feeling guilt. And then I had to wonder.

If that's how they treated someone so kind and sweet as Sister Claire, why would I ever want to become a nun?

1968 SPRING SURPRISE

During the winter months in New England we skied, skated and spent many hours tobogganing on the snow and ice. As we entered elementary school my parents enrolled each of their children in skiing class. Free lessons were sponsored by the city for the locals every Friday night beginning in January and most families took advantage. At the time, I resented the hours spent riding the rope tow and doing the Stem-Christie maneuvers over and over again in the frigid temps but the lessons eventually paid off. My childhood was spent, every year, winter after winter, at the local ski area, Mt. Chamber. The place became a hangout for Ellen and me.

In February 1968 a Northeaster dumped 18 inches of fresh powdery snow on the slopes. With school vacation in full swing Mt. Chamber was crowded as hundreds of children combed the ski area. The mountain provided trails from novice to expert. Rope tows and chair lifts ran constantly from sunrise to sunset. One morning during vacation week Ellen and I stopped for a rest midpoint on Barrel Run, one of the intermediate ski trails.

"Hello brats!"

With a deep swoosh, Steven swished by covering us with a light spray of snow.

"Ugh!! Steven!!" I yelled as I shook the snow from my ski hat and wiped my face.

He was nothing but trouble. Seconds later, two girls from St. Timothy's came slowly down the mountain to join us. Holly and Mary Jane were fairly new to the sport, having learned to ski only that winter. They took their time carefully trekking down the slope, steering away from any large moguls. I watched nervously as a group of five or six boys raced to join Steven, who was just a short distance from us. They whooped and hollered as they skied back and forth across the trail getting dangerously close to Mary Jane, who didn't see them approaching.

It all happened in a matter of seconds.

One of the boys' skis caught the edge of Mary Jane's. The two tumbled several feet down the hill, their skis entangled and ski poles flying. Immediately there was an anguished cry of pain. I could see Mary Jane's right leg was bent at a very peculiar angle. Her perpetrator, however, was uninjured.

"Go get help!" I shouted to Steven as I quickly side stepped my way to help the girl.

Surprisingly, without hesitation, he took off like a shot down the mountain and the ski patrol rescue team arrived within minutes.

Mary Jane suffered a broken tibia which meant a cast for eight weeks.

When we returned to school a week later Sister Bridgette was frantic about how to handle the situation with Mary Jane. Because her cast encased her entire leg from thigh to toes she would require assistance in every aspect of her school day. Sister surveyed the classroom as she contemplated on who she would designate to help. Someone would have to be willing to sacrifice to be at Mary Jane's beck and call. It would mean giving up lunches and recesses with friends.

"Maureen! To the front please."

My shoulders dropped. Annoyed, I sighed and slowly approached Sister's desk. As much as I liked Mary Jane I didn't look forward to being attached to the girl for the next several weeks.

"Yes, Sister?"

"Maureen, I'd like you to assist Mary Jane until further notice. You may leave a few minutes early to go downstairs to the cafeteria to get both of your lunches, but of course you will eat here and recess will be here in the classroom. And remember, you will have to help Mary Jane with any personal issues, such as going to the lavatory."

Oh, Lord I thought to myself. It's going to be a long winter. I wished I had the courage to argue with Bugsy.

"Yes, Sister."

For the next two weeks I enjoyed getting our lunch trays and bringing them back up to the classroom. Since the friendly cafeteria ladies felt sorry for Mary Jane they made sure to include an extra dessert on each of our trays.

The extra helping of apple crisp or chocolate pudding seemed to make it worthwhile.

But eventually our lunch together became boring. I couldn't believe Sister Bridgette trusted us to be by ourselves for the entire lunch period. Sister went to the cafeteria with the rest of the class and never once returned to check on us, which turned out to be a blessing. Some days after eating, we played cards or a game of hangman. I even got brave enough to draw funny pictures on the blackboard, making sure to have everything erased by 12:25 pm.

But by the fourth week I was going stir crazy. Mary Jane was a bookworm and was content reading her series of Bobbsey Twin books, but I had too much energy. Making small talk while eating lunch in the classroom every day felt like drudgery. I wanted to be outside with my other friends playing a game of tag or sliding down the church ramp. And I was tired of running down three flights of stairs to get our lunches only to have to go back downstairs to return the empty trays.

One day after finishing my meal, but not ready to make the trek back to the cafeteria, I wandered over to one of the large windows.

It was a cold gray day outside but I opened the window about four inches and breathed in the crisp fresh air. It smelled like a snowstorm approaching. I watched various people go inside the rundown market located directly across the street. It was a shabby decrepit store located on the banks of the river that connected two of the many lakes in the area.

I'd heard from other kids that the store sold dirty magazines, displayed right at the front counter, along with beer, cigarettes and other groceries. I suspected that's why my parents told me to stay away from the place. Several boys from school, including Steven, claimed to have gone inside to buy penny candy but everyone speculated as to why they were really going.

Snowflakes began to fall again and would bring another foot of the white stuff.

My gaze turned to the convent located right next to the school. Although separate, the two buildings were built extremely close together with just a very narrow walking path separating them. Several times I had been given the opportunity to go there, not by choice, to deliver notes from Sister Bridgette.

It was as though she knew how much I disliked going to the convent. Whenever she asked me to do the task I visibly cringed.

The building was foreboding, with an enormous wrap-around porch and heavily draped windows on either side of the front entrance. Each time I quietly approached the door and rang the bell I looked around, ready to run but inevitably someone would answer. Like out of a scary movie, the creaky door opened ever so slowly. Immediately I could smell the inside of the house. The distinct stale odor, not a pleasant one, was one I recognized whenever the nuns stood close to me. The entry was dark making it difficult to see the tiny shriveled up old lady dressed in a gray uniform. I avoided looking at the housekeeper's face as I quickly handed her the sealed envelope and retreated down the front steps without saying a word.

As I raced down the porch steps a shrill voice called out to me, "Miss, would you like to come in?"

A shiver went up my spine as I pretended not to hear her and quickened my step. I was thankful to get back into school.

The Victorian building's paint was chipped and faded gold and had enormous floor to ceiling lace covered windows. The windows on the second floor were covered with heavy dark drapes and I wondered what could possibly be behind them. Perhaps the nuns' bedrooms? Or could they be secret rooms where the nuns were sent for punishment? My imagination ran wild.

Directly below our classroom window was the convent's porch roof. It was covered with pristine white snow and I surmised from all of the recent storms the pile had to be at least a two feet deep.

That's when the idea came to me.

I went over and scooped up my empty lunch tray and returned to the window, opened it a bit wider and leaned my head out.

"Geez, Maureen, close the window! I'm freezing!"

Mary Jane began to whine but her voice quickly changed when she saw what I was up to.

"Are you crazy? Are you really going to do that? Sister's going to kill you!"

I spun around and snapped, "Not if she doesn't find out!"

"I want to watch. Hang on, let me see!"

I waited as Mary Jane grabbed her crutches and hobbled over next to me. After glancing over my shoulder to be sure the coast was clear, I knelt on the radiator and leaned further out the window. I closed one eye and aimed for a spot directly in the center of the roof. The tray landed quietly and deeply in the snow. Any tracks would be completely hidden with the additional falling flurries.

Throughout the next four weeks I periodically returned trays to the lunch room, only to keep the cafeteria ladies from becoming suspicious. With Mary Jane joining me at the window, fears of her tattling to Bugsy completely disappeared. In fact the practice became the highlight of Mary Jane's recuperation.

By late March her cast was off and my school day returned to normal. Mary Jane and I forgot about the trays and never spoke of them again, until one afternoon when Bugsy summoned Mr. Lachant, the school janitor to our classroom.

My accomplice and I exchanged glances as the nun and the simple-minded man peered out the window to the roof below. Mr. Lachant scratched his head and said he couldn't fathom how those things ended up on the convent roof, Sista. And wasn't it unfortunate, Sista, that you didn't have proof of who done it.

The suspicious nun slowly shook her head and scanned the class out of the corner of her accusing fish eye. My heart beat rapidly in my chest as I watched and waited.

Inside I was smiling.

But outside I remained as solemn as a nun.

1968 NEVER ENOUGH BLESSINGS

If there was one thing I knew about going to mass so frequently it was that I certainly felt protected by an unseen higher power. There was always one reason or another to go to church for a special blessing—a holy day of obligation when we professed our faith and reconfirmed our baptism vows or a feast of one saint or another where we participated in the ritual that would protect us from harm.

February 1968 was a busy month for blessings. It began on the 4th with the feast of St. Blaise. We celebrated the saint's life by attending mass and having our throats blessed by the priest. The story was told that the saint saved a young boy from choking on a fish bone, or at least that's what my mother told me. And being that it was cold and flu season, she felt it was important for us to attend mass and receive the unique blessing from the priest.

"You can never get enough blessings, Maureen. It's very important to get this one to protect you from choking and sore throats."

I didn't care what she said, I still didn't like it.

At the end of mass, instead of leaving church, the congregation lined up in the middle aisle as though going to communion. One by one we approached the priest at the altar. As I stood in front of him he placed two cream colored candles criss-crossed around my neck—that alone made me feel as though I was choking. My eyes crossed as I looked down at his hairy knuckles holding the candles that rested on either side of my throat and I listened to his mumbled prayer. Once he removed the candles I made the sign of the cross and quickly headed to the side door while rubbing my neck. I had the sensation that the candles were still closing in on my throat.

My mother smiled, relieved that each of her children would be protected from any throat ailments for the coming year.

February was also the time for preparation of the next big church holiday, Easter. The nuns pestered us about sacrificing something for Lent, which began on Ash Wednesday. During each religion class Sister Bridgette talked about giving up food or an activity that was important to us, something we would miss greatly, as a way to prepare our hearts and clean our souls for Easter. For forty days and forty nights until April 14th I had to think about and resist temptation of something that meant a lot to me. I contemplated chocolate or snacking after school. But I knew Bugsy meant to sacrifice something like television. However, I knew in my heart I would never make it to Easter without cheating, I had too many favorite shows to watch.

Of course she suggested we add extra prayers and rosaries as part of our Lenten reflection. And I agreed to do so. But I knew I probably would not follow through every day.

She reiterated that fish was the meal of choice on Ash Wednesday, and meat was forbidden on Fridays during Lent. That was okay with me as I looked forward to my mother's famous tuna wiggle on toast for supper on Friday nights.

On February 28 1968 the nuns prepared to take their classes to the Ash Wednesday mass. Of course I had to ready myself and also Mary Jane, who was on crutches. Thankfully, the sidewalks were clear and the two of us maneuvered over to the church safely and smoothly. Mary Jane moved swiftly as I tagged along behind her, but going up the church steps was tricky. They were made of thick granite and even without crutches you got a work out climbing them. I held her crutches and her left arm as she grabbed the rail and slowly hopped up on one foot, a step at a time. Sister had given us a head start before the others so there was no need to rush. Once inside we waited for our classmates to arrive then followed Bugsy down the center aisle. The mass was a regular one and just like the feast of St Blaise, the blessing was given out at the very end.

Steven, who was sitting next to Mary Jane, fidgeted the entire hour. Periodically he knocked on her cast, and asked if she could feel the tapping.

"No, now stop it" she whispered. Suddenly he began to play with one of her crutches. Before she could stop him he picked it up and pointed it like a rifle. Sister Bridgette quickly climbed over Patrick and Francis, and as she stood on the kneeler, whacked Steven over the head with a church song book. Unbeknownst to Sister, Francis leaned far back in the pew in disgust and made comical motions towards Bugsy's rear end which only caused laughter amongst the surrounding pews. Even adults attending the mass chuckled at the boy's antics. Steven rubbed the back of his head and was silent until mass was over.

We stood in line and processed to the altar to receive our ashes. Father dipped his thick thumb into the tiny bowl of damp ashes then made the sign of the cross on my forehead. I felt bits and pieces of the dark stuff fall onto my nose and cheeks as he mumbled a prayer about 'ashes to ashes and dust we shall return'. When he finished I made the sign of the cross and returned to the pew, per Sister's instructions. Each of us looked at one another and giggled. Smudges of gray ash appeared on our foreheads, right between the eyes. Many of us had sprinkles of the stuff across our noses and cheeks. But I remembered what Sister Bridgette told us earlier.

"Do not wipe off any of the ashes! They have been blessed and are meant to stay on until they wear off on their own."

She was serious and we believed her. We left the smudges on our faces and did not to wash them off. It could take days for the dark spot to disappear.

Everyone looked as though they'd been sitting too close to a bonfire. There was no escaping the fact that we were Catholic and had participated in the Ash Wednesday ritual.

While walking home later that day I received lots of strange looks from non-Catholics. But I also spotted fellow parishioners which made me feel as though we had a secret connection, belonged to a special club.

And it was obvious to me they'd been given instructions about washing their ashes off as well.

I felt special as they'd give a slight nod and maybe a smile as they recognized me as a dutiful Catholic girl.

And that was a blessing.

1968 THE MAY PROCESSION

On the evening of the annual May procession Principal Xavier slowly paced the gym observing the entire student body. Back and forth she strolled with her beady eyes scanning us from head to toe. Her mission was to be sure every child was dressed appropriately. Boys were required to wear dress shirts, ties and preferably a sports jacket. Most everyone I knew wore their church outfit left over from Easter Sunday.

Girls were required to cover their heads. Some girls wore rectangular white mantillas that looked like a miniature table cloth. I chose the up-to-date white covering which was small and circular and looked like a table doily plopped on the top of my head. All of our dresses had to be the appropriate length—nothing above the knee. I was so grateful to my Grammy Fitzpatrick for buying me a beautiful mint green chiffon dress. The color went well with my hair and the length was perfect. My only problem was that it was sleeveless. Although I was 12 ½ my mother would not allow me to shave the wispy growth that was sprouting under my arms and on my calves. I loved the dress and wanted to wear it so I had hopes my mother would change her mind.

Right up until the day of the procession I argued with my mother, but she remained adamant and rejected my request to shave. I had no choice. I hated to cover the pretty dress but I donned a white cardigan to hide the light brown wisps under my arms and pulled on my highest white knee socks in hopes of hiding the dark hair on my legs. Unfortunately for me this beautiful day in May turned unseasonably warm and I had to deflect questions as to why I was wearing a sweater. I claimed I was chilled, perhaps coming down with a spring cold or hay fever which seemed to quell my mother's curiosity.

Satisfied with our appearance, Principal Xavier nodded to Sister Bridgette, giving the signal to begin. Bugsy took charge by clapping her hands as she waddled around the gym.

Considered a very special occasion, the procession celebrated the Blessed Virgin Mary, mother of God. With the entire student body participating in the event, weeks of preparation had taken place. The entire school had practiced the specially selected hymns over and over again. The eighth grade class had crafted a large blue and white banner depicting a picture of Mary that would be carried in the front of the procession.

Every day for weeks, we filed down to the gym after lunch to practice. The nuns lined us up according to height. I ended up near the end of the line paired up with Francis O'Neal. He was a comical boy who was a bit rambunctious. Francis always looked sloppy with messy hair and stains on his uniformed shirt, but somehow he still looked cute. He didn't cuss like Steven but like his classmate, he was a jokester and liked to push the limits with the nuns.

On the evening of the procession Francis looked cuter than ever. He was scrubbed clean with his hair neatly combed and his crisp white shirt tucked into pressed khakis. My stomach fluttered as we took our designated places.

Since Ellen was the tallest girl in class she was once again given the privilege of crowning the statue of the Blessed Mother in church. Unfortunately for her, she had to walk at the far end of the procession with the group of nuns. As much as I would have loved a chance of putting the crown on Mary I was grateful to be walking with my classmates.

"Attention! Attention! Everyone get in your places!" Bugsy shouted.

We lined up and put our palms together in prayer. With the unusually humid air the temperature in the gymnasium was climbing. Some children began fanning themselves, only to be scolded by Sister Bridgette. I tried my best to stay cool, but I could feel the perspiration building under my sweater.

"Quiet everyone! Quiet!" Principal Xavier called out in her quivering voice.

"Man, I don't think she's going to make it to church!" whispered Francis. "The old crow must be at least 100 years old!"

I smirked at his comment but was not taking any chances of being reprimanded, Bugsy was standing too close.

Sister Bridgette waved to the music teacher, Sister Claire, who was standing on a folding chair. The young nun held one hand up to get our attention. Everyone quieted down as she blew into the pitch pipe giving us the starting note for the first hymn, "*Salve Regina*".

Principal Xavier slowly led the parade through the large gym doors, up the stairs and out into the school yard. Slowly and methodically she stepped, turning around every minute or so to be sure we stayed in formation. Directly behind her, two teen aged boys carried the procession banner. The entire student body sang the hymn as we headed over to church. Sister Alexander, Sister Claire, Sister Dympna and Sister Oliver took their appointed places alongside the processional to ensure everyone stayed in line with hands folded in prayer. Sister Bridgette made it her mission to stroll up and down the line making sure we walked together, two by two, behaving precisely the way she wanted. Sister Xavier led the student body across the parking lot/play area of the school, down the driveway and around to the front door of the 100 year old church. Hundreds of parents, grandparents and family members stood along the processional route. They nodded solemnly to the nuns then waved excitedly to their children as they snapped pictures with their Polaroid cameras.

The heat was causing my arms to itch and my cheeks were hot. I just knew that they were glowing red.

As we approached the front I was relieved to see large fans set up on the altar. I hoped my seat would be in line with the breeze. I knew I couldn't do anything about my hair, which was becoming curlier by the minute. I tried not to think about it as I continued down the aisle singing "*Immaculate Mary*."

We finished singing and waited in our appropriate pews, while Ellen approached the life sized statue of the Blessed Mother, located next to the altar. The organist played soft background music as Ellen carried the crown of flowers crafted by Sister Margaret, the school's art teacher. The circle was composed of fresh violets, pink rose buds, and lily of the valley. Ellen handed the crown to Sister Xavier, who stood nearby to assist. Once on the stepstool, she steadied herself while Sister Xavier handed her the crown. Holding the ring of flowers, Ellen stretched as high as she could. The motion caused her lemon flowered dress to lift as she reached toward Mary's head.

I covered my mouth in horror as I watched the half slip slide from beneath her dress and slowly creep down her legs. Poor Ellen! If only I could have run over and put her slip back into place. Out of instinct, Ellen reached down with one hand to snatch her slip back into position. But when she did she lost her footing on the stepstool.

The next 30 seconds happened as if in slow motion. Ellen struggled with her undergarment and found herself leaning towards the large statue of the Blessed Mother. To avoid knocking the icon over she let go of the crown which caused her to tumble off the stool. Sister Xavier reached to help, but the sudden force caused the elderly woman to stumble back and land on her rear end—with Ellen precisely on top of her.

The parents gasped. Students laughed. Nuns rushed to the front to untangle the two. Sister Bridgette tried desperately to stop the laughter. Ellen was face to face with Sister Xavier, who was huffing and puffing, gasping for air. Each time Ellen struggled to stand up she put pressure on the nun's belly.

"I think she squished the shit outta her!" Steven declared as he stood on the pew to watch.

"The old crow can't breathe!!"

Father Murphy, who had been observing from the altar, ran over to help the two to their feet. After confirming that the nun was fine he quickly tossed the crown of flowers atop of Mary's head and continued with mass.

Ellen was near tears as she returned to her seat.

"Hell of a move, Callahan!" Steven remarked as she passed by. "Way to kill the principal!"

Ellen ignored his remark while Sister Xavier smoothed her habit and continued on as though nothing had occurred. Father Murphy returned to the altar and began his lengthy homily. The ritual concluded with a recitation of the Hail Mary.

After returning to the school gymnasium, cookies and fruit punch were served by the parish Ladies' Guild while families and students milled about.

I was sweltering.

There were drops of sweat rolling down the sides of my face and my sweater was making me itch. As soon as our parents began chatting with Sister Xavier Ellen and I snuck away to the girl's lavatory. Both of us had had enough. As I tore off my sweater to cool off Ellen removed her slip and threw it into the trash bin.

Latching our pinky fingers together, we swore that next year things would be different. But I knew one thing had to change, and change fast, despite everything my mother said.

The following afternoon, my best friend and I borrowed her father's double edged razor and locked ourselves in the bathroom.

1968 A CLOSE CALL

L ike most school cafeterias St. Timothy's lunch room overflowed with the sound of children's chatter and the clanging of lunch trays. It was the place to share stories and gossip while eating a wholesome hot lunch. Once a week the nuns allowed students to leave the school grounds and go home for lunch. Often times I walked the short distance to have lunch with Grammy Fitzpatrick. She worked as a secretary at a local office that was just around the corner from the school. Time spent with Grammy and her fellow co-workers was precious to me. I felt independent as I ventured out on my own to the office building.

If I didn't have plans for lunch with Grammy my mother usually packed my meal in a brown paper bag. The wonderful smells from the cafeteria were enticing as I ate my peanut butter and grape jelly sandwich. I cherished the days when my mom could scrape together the sixty five cents for me to buy one of the delicious hot lunches.

In the small but adequate kitchen the friendly cafeteria ladies prepared and served home-cooked meals. With limited resources the crew managed to create delicious dishes like sloppy joes, real mashed potatoes and gravy, and sweet apple crisp with whipped cream for dessert.

Beginning in the month of May, when the weather was warmer, the nuns allowed us to take our lunches outside. Usually on a Friday, the lunch ladies prepared sandwiches—egg salad, tuna salad or cold meat—wrapped neatly in wax paper, a small bag of Wise potato chips, and two generous homemade chocolate chip cookies along with a pint-sized carton of milk packed in a paper bag.

Once outside we were allowed to choose any place to eat in the playground/parking lot. I looked forward to these spring picnics, since we could separate ourselves from the ever-present nuns. Oh, they would still monitor us. But there were so many segregated little groups on the playground that they were spread quite thin.

At the very back of the parking lot was a thick line of pine trees that hid a very steep grassy slope. At the bottom of that hill were railroad tracks.

Each day at approximately 11:45 a.m., a B & M train chugged along the tracks. We became used to the familiar rhythmic sound of the train and the loud drawn out whistle as it approached the crossing at Church and Main St. just a block away.

Our playground was not fenced in but everyone was aware of the boundaries. Each year we were reminded of where we were to play. The nuns repeated the story of two teen-aged boys who had played down near the railroad tracks some twenty years before. One had dared the other to jump onto the train as it passed by St. Timothy's. As the huge engine slowed down and began its daily approach to the next railroad crossing the boys thought they'd be able to outrun the train and have ample time to climb aboard. One leaped from the grass as he tried to land on the caboose. But as he clung to the rail on the side of the train, his legs became entangled in the undercarriage of the boxcar. His screams could not be heard above the noisy locomotive. Horrified, his friend ran as fast as he could to the front of the train, pleading for it to stop. But by the time the engineer glanced out the side window and saw the boy's friend, it was too late.

In my three years at St. Timothy's I had never seen anyone attempt to go beyond the trees or venture toward the tracks. It was a story the nuns told us over and over again, I suspect, to scare us and keep us from going beyond the boundary, down the slope or anywhere near the train.

On Thursday May 16, 1968, someone didn't remember the story.

The sky was brilliantly blue that spring day. The fresh warm air welcomed colorful butterflies and fat yellow and black bumble bees as white clovers sprouted throughout the grassy areas. My friend Ellen and I found a quiet spot just in front of a thick clump of trees along the backside of the parking lot. The grass had not been mowed and was cushiony and lush to stretch out on. We unpacked our lunch bags and began to eat our egg salad sandwiches.

"I have to tell you about Davy Jones!" Ellen exclaimed. She had just finished reading the latest *Tiger Beat* magazine the night before. Just as she began we heard the familiar sound of the locomotive.

Ellen paused, waiting for the whistle to stop then picked up right where she left off.

"So, they showed pictures of where he grew up, over in England!"

She was interrupted again when Steven and Francis came too close to our sandwiches.

The boys were playing tag instead of eating their lunches.

"Hey, watch out! You almost stepped on my cookies!"

I yelled but he kept on going, chasing Francis round and round our area, who was laughing and out of breath as he tried to keep away from Steven. Francis ran amongst the trees then stopped at the top of the slope, just for a second, to catch his breath. Steven lunged toward him and began to chase him down the hill. When I saw the boys disappear over the top I jumped up and ran over to see if they had gone any further. I couldn't believe my eyes. Sure enough, Steven was chasing his friend down the grassy slope. Before I knew it Francis' feet were up in the air as he began to tumble backwards.

"Francis!!" I screamed frantically.

Sister Xavier, who happened to be close by, lumbered as fast as she could to see what was happening.

"What's going on here? Oh my Lord! Oh my Jesus!"

Steven stopped half way down the hill and stood still as he watched his friend roll quickly down the grass, heading right for the train tracks. Ellen and I ran to Steven. We could hear the locomotive approaching.

"Oh no, Steven! Do something!!" I cried as my heart pounded.

Sister began her descent down the hill. I couldn't take my eyes off of Francis, who was rolling dangerously close to the tracks.

"Hurry Sister!" Ellen shouted to the feeble nun.

Suddenly out of nowhere Sister Claire leaped from behind us and raced down the hill. She held her black habit up above her knees as she sprinted towards Francis. The train was now visible.

The engineer leaned out of the window waving his hand frantically. He was shouting but we couldn't hear what he was saying. I covered my ears as he blew the loud whistle several more times.

The two women continued down the hill, Sister Claire zoomed past her fellow nun.

"Francis!!"

Sister Xavier screamed just before she fell. The momentum had been too much for her. Her rounded body lurched forward and down she went. She did at least two somersaults before landing just behind Sister Claire. The brakes on the enormous engine screeched so loud I had to cover my ears.

Francis came to a stop dangerously close to the tracks with his right arm resting across the steel rail.

I squeezed my eyes shut for a few seconds and prayed Please God, help him!

Sister Claire reached Francis in the nick of time. With two hands she grabbed the waist of his khakis and pulled him away from the oncoming train. The engineer stopped the locomotive just several yards away.

Francis began to sob. Steven looked like he'd seen a ghost as he turned and scampered back up the hill as fast as he could. Sister Claire brushed the strands of grass off Francis' back as he steadied himself on his feet. The pounding of my heart subsided. That was just way too close.

Sister Xavier was laying face down. Her black habit was twisted up to her knees with her veil lifted to the top of her head. I gasped as I could see her white locks twisted up into a very tight bun. The nun's cheek rested on the grass squishing her face in the white headpiece.

"Sister, are you okay?" Sister Claire ran to assist a woozy Sister Xavier. She adjusted the nun's habit and veil and helped her to her feet.

"Perhaps you should sit down for a minute" Sister Claire suggested. But Sister Xavier was stubborn and would have none of it. She waved the younger nun away then straightened her dress, pulled at the headpiece to loosen it from her jaw and began her slow ascent up the hill without uttering a single word.

Although she was limping she steadfastly refused any assistance. By now a crowd had formed at the top of the slope. Sister Bridgette immediately began to usher everyone away.

"It's all over now, children. Go back to your lunch. Everyone is fine."

Ellen and I went back to our spot and sat quietly as we finished our sandwiches. In fact, most of the students were subdued for the rest of the afternoon. We had all learned a valuable lesson that day.

For the next two weeks the playground remained closed. We were not allowed to play outside while the contractors installed the new fence.

The entire week after the train incident Sister Xavier remained in the convent recuperating from her fall. Sister Bridgette took on the role of St. Timothy's acting principal.

Little did we know that her interim position would eventually become a permanent one.

1969 CHOIR PRACTICE

From my first days at St. Timothy's I dreamed of singing in the school choir. The thought of sitting high above the altar in the loft intrigued me. At each Sunday mass I stole glances behind me as I looked up to where the choir sat. I could see familiar faces from my school dressed in their forest green choir gowns. Their voices were beautiful and I looked forward to when I would be eligible to try out.

I was twelve in 1969 and music was becoming an important part of my life. The local A.M. station played the top tunes and I cranked up the one small radio we had at home to listen to them. Ellen and I saved our allowance and any babysitting money we earned to buy records at JJ Newberry's, the local department store. Every weekend we played our small 45's over and over again on Ellen's record player, as we memorized the lyrics and practiced the latest dance moves we had seen on *American Bandstand*. Each of us took turns singing the lead of songs by *The Monkees* and *Paul Revere* and *the Raiders*. On Saturday afternoons we forced our younger siblings to watch our performances in Ellen's basement. When the kids whined and complained we handed out dimes to bribe them to sit and listen to our full rendition of *Sugar Sugar* and *Dizzy*.

By the time we heard about the choir tryouts in September, Ellen and I felt confident and ready to audition. Along with our favorite pop tunes, we had rehearsed the familiar hymns from mass.

Sister Bridgette, now the official principal of St. Timothy's, still held her position as a teacher in the classroom and was also in charge of choir auditions. During class several students questioned her about the songs we would be asked to sing but she remained silent. I noticed with each passing year Bugsy became more and more ornery and it reflected in her personality at school.

On the day of tryouts a mix of excitement and nerves fluttered in my belly as I made my way to the music room after school. I cleared my dry throat numerous times while making countless trips to the water bubbler. Lyrics from the many hymns I'd memorized went round and round in my head as I knew Sister Bridgette would be offended if I forgot any of the words to the all too familiar songs. As I joined Ellen at the back of the classroom, I wiped my sweaty palms across my uniform and smoothed the untamed curls around my face.

"Look at Bugsy's sourpuss! She sure looks angry." Ellen whispered as I took a spot next to her.

"I don't know what that old crow's problem is."

I glanced across the room to where the nun was talking with Sister Claire. Sister Bridgette's face had a scowl, as though she had a bad taste in her mouth.

"This ought to be fun." I responded under my breath. "But I refuse to let her intimidate me."

All told there were 15 other students trying out. None of us knew how many spots were open or how many Sister would be choosing. Sister Claire appeared peaceful and at ease as she practiced on the piano while Sister Bridgette fussed with her clipboard and made her way to the back of the room. A beautiful melody played which I recognized right away. It was *Come Holy Ghost, Creator Blest*. Immediately I remembered the words to the hymn and went over them in my mind.

"MARY JOOOO!" Sister Bridgette bellowed which startled Sister Claire so much she abruptly removed her hands from the keys.

Eighth grader Mary Jo McMann sashayed across the room and stood next to the antique upright piano. She looked over and smiled at Sister Bridgette who then blew into the pitch pipe and raised her hand signaling Sister Claire to begin.

"Cooooome, Hooolyyy, Ghooooost! Creeeeeator Bleeessst!"

Mary Jo began singing softly. Her voice became stronger as she belted out the words effortlessly and on key. At the tremendous crescendo Sister Bridgette beamed with pride and joy at Mary Jo. It wasn't often Bugsy smiled. Everyone knew that Mary Jo was a wonderful singer. After all, she always had a lead role in all of the school's variety shows. So it was a bit intimidating to say the least, which made me wonder if that was ultimately Sister's motive.

"What the hell is that about? Everyone knows that Mary Jo can sing like a stupid canary." Ellen leaned in and whispered. "I think Sister is trying to scare us off."

"Of course she is! Mary Jo's the pet, for sure. Sister thinks we'll change our minds about trying out."

"Well, that's horseshit because I will STILL audition just to spite the old crow!"

We watched Mary Jo finish her performance with her head tilted back and her eyes gazed up to the ceiling. She clasped her hands together then clutched them dramatically to her chest. Ellen and I looked at one another and began to giggle. The girl looked as though she were possessed by the devil.

"Let's do exactly what she's doing!!" I whispered to Ellen as I lifted my chin and rolled my eyes back in my head. Ellen unsuccessfully stifled a laugh.

"She looks like she's in rapture!"

When the song ended Sister Bridgette clapped her hands in excitement and glided over to Mary Jo.

"Wonderful! Just wonderful! As usual your voice was like that of an angel."

Mary Jo blushed as Sister patted her on the top of the head as though she were a dog. Sister told her to return to the rest of the group then she scanned her clipboard.

"Okay, let's see here. Miss Mulldoon, you're next."

The nun's demeanor quickly changed and her voice was somber. I certainly didn't feel the welcome she had just expressed to Mary Jo.

Sister Bridgette sauntered over to the opposite side of the classroom, tossed the clipboard on desk, defiantly folded her arms and raised her hand to signal to Sister Claire. She didn't bother using the pitch pipe for me. Sister Claire played a few notes.

I thought I was ready. I took several deep breaths and closed my eyes. I don't what happened but nothing was coming out of my mouth. I knew I wanted this! I wanted to wear a green choir gown!

My face was getting hot and my mouth was very dry.

I glanced over at Sister Claire who nodded to me and offered a compassionate gesture with her eyes that said, 'Relax'. I lowered my eyes and focused on the desk in front of me. I didn't tilt my head back or clasp my hands to my chest. Instead I gripped small handfuls on either side of my plaid skirt. With eyes cast down I could block out the others waiting their turn. I didn't want to look at Bugsy. I couldn't even look at Ellen.

"Come Hoooly Ghoooost, Creaaaator Blest...."

I began to relax.

I barely finished the first verse when Sister Bridgette interrupted me.

"Okay, okay! That's enough. Thank you, Maureen."

She waved her hand in the air signaling for me to stop as she waddled over to the piano.

"You can get back in line."

I couldn't believe her rudeness. I was mortified. Bugsy was undoubtedly playing favorites. My mind was busy with all kinds of responses to give her. That was a really shitty thing to do Sister, an awful thing to do! But I swallowed my anger without uttering a word and turned and walked away.

"You sounded super! You just HAVE to make it! Just forget about that old witch," Ellen whispered.

I shrugged my shoulders and leaned against the wall relieved it was over but I couldn't shake the feeling that Sister Bridgette really had it in for me. I could barely look at the nun.

The next day after the final bell, I was nervous as I ran to view the list of newly selected choir members posted just outside the music room. With one finger running down the long list of names, I scanned the paper and found Ellen's name midway down. Relieved that they were not in alphabetical order I finally saw my name near the bottom of the list. Maureen Mulldoon—Alto.

We could finally wear the green gowns!

Our first practice was the following Saturday morning. As instructed by Sister Bridgette, the group met in the back of the church at 9 a.m. Sister Claire stood in the doorway and greeted each of us with a cheerful hello, while Sister Bridgette sent out a gruff good morning as she gave us the once over before leading us up the back stairs of the church.

The steep wooden stairs leading to the loft were very narrow and twisted round and round. I couldn't imagine how Sister maneuvered her fat self up there.

As I stepped through the tiny doorway at the top of the stairs the space felt very magical and mysterious. The high wooden rafters creaked and cracked. Dim lighting from a large antique chandelier cast a soft glow. The area was not as big as I had once believed. Six wooden pews were placed stadium style, with the last row set directly in front of the gigantic stained glass window. Anyone with a fear of heights would have found it difficult to make their way to the top. The last row was only a few feet away from the peak of the roof but had a bird's eye view of the entire loft and church. The enormous pipe organ sat against the right side of the loft. As I looked out to the church the altar appeared to be miles away.

I peered over the railing and looked down on the pews below. It was a long way down.

I recalled a story my mother had told me about a flying bat in church. Several years before, during a Holy Day mass, a screeching bat had flown around the loft. Choir members screamed and cried right in the middle of the communion song. The interruption caused the nun to stop playing, the singers to stop singing and the entire hymn was ruined. Sister Bridgette had an angry fit and punished everyone by making them scrub each and every pew in the church after school the next day. From then on it was passed on to all choir members to be on high alert for any flying creatures.

Each of our practices lasted two hours, without any breaks. Sister Bridgette was a perfectionist and expected her students to perform the hymns flawlessly. She constantly interrupted Sister Claire.

"No, no,no!! Now let's start again. Girls, yoooouuuu MUST sing louder! Father will not hear a thing down on the altar. Now, AGAIN!!"

And so we sang and sang until our throats were sore by the time we went home.

Our first mass was within two weeks. Dressed proudly in freshly pressed choir gowns and carrying our hymnals we climbed the spiral staircase to the loft. My alto alternate position required me to sit with the other altos, mostly boys, to the far left in the last row. I was far removed from Sister Bridgette, who took her place at the railing and faced us. As I looked down, I followed Sister Claire's hands as they swiftly moved across the keys of the organ. Looking further, I observed the priest and altar boys, who looked miniature on the altar. As mass went on each of the songs were performed perfectly.

It was during the final hymn just after Eucharist when something caught my eye. It fluttered quickly above my head then swooped down close to the top of Sister Claire's veil. She was oblivious as she continued to play her music. I wasn't sure what to do. Others around me also witnessed the flying creature and cranked their necks to watch it as we continued to sing. The bat whooshed by and I could hear the soft flutter of its wings. As it became agitated it picked up momentum and dipped close to the rail, circled back up again then headed straight for me. I ducked my head down and stopped singing as I began to laugh nervously. Others around me stopped singing as well and watched as the bat frantically searched for an exit.

Sister Bridgette didn't have a clue. She was lost in the moment as she conducted her choir. The nun's eyes were closed as her raised arms swayed back and forth in time with the music. She had no idea that her conducting was enticing the winged creature. Once again the bat swooped right over Bugsy's head then suddenly veered in for a landing. Apparently it was drawn to Sister Bridgette's billowy long black sleeves. She was oblivious as the bat latched on and clung to her left arm. Even while it fluttered its wings against her, she continued to wave her arms to the beat of the hymn. When the song came to an end, Sister's arms fell to her sides. It was at that moment the bat frantically tried to make its escape by flapping its wings. Janie jumped up from the front row and reached out to the nun.

"Sister, there's a bat!!"

Sister Bridgette looked down at her sleeve and began to scream hysterically. She shook her arm wildly as she tried to dislodge the creature. Those in the front row sat with their eyes wide as saucers and their mouths open in horror. Sister Claire stopped playing and turned around to see what the fuss was about.

Bugsy spun in circles as she tried to shake the bat off her sleeve. Within seconds she stumbled and reeled backwards. Before anyone could stop her she was on her back on the wooden rail as her legs straddled the railing. Hearing the screams and commotion, parishioners seated directly below looked up at the choir loft. Rumblings and gasps could be heard as the crowd turned around to watch the nun struggle to release the bat and avoid falling on the people below.

"Hold on Sister!"

One gentleman jumped up and made his way through the crowd.

Sister Bridgette began to cry. Gravity had taken over causing her black habit to creep downwards. Her left shoe swung wildly back and forth over the parishioners. The nun's protruding belly and extra weight prevented her from sitting up on her own. Her long black veil hung precariously over the railing. Each time she tried to bring herself upright her head piece became askew.

None of us moved. We all watched, not knowing whether to laugh or cry. A quick thinking Sister Claire jumped up from the organ to assist.

"Sister! Give me your hand!"

But Sister Bridgette wasn't listening as she continued to battle the bat that was still clinging to her sleeve. It had no intention of letting go.

"Someone help me get Sister!" Sister Claire shouted to the choir. "Steven, boys hurry!!"

Steven, who was sitting several rows up, slowly climbed down to assist the two nuns. He hesitated and looked scared. After all, it was SISTER BRIDGETTE! He motioned to his buddies, but no one offered their help. He was alone with this one.

"Hellllp!"

Sister Bridgette's voice grew faint and she looked as though she was about to pass out.

Steven took a deep breath and along with Sister Claire grabbed the nun's flailing arm and yanked as hard as they could. The motion turned her stocky body upside down so that both of her legs were now atop the rail and her head almost hit the loft floor. Steven grabbed a hymnal and slammed it against the bat. The force released the creature and it flew off towards the altar.

Parishioners gasped as they watched the bat fly around the church. They quickly began to exit the building.

It only took one person.

Someone seated down below began laughing and pointing at the upside nun, which caused everyone else to look up. Sister Bridgette's legs were completely exposed and her feet were straight up in the air. Her black nun's habit crept slowly towards the floor revealing almost everything underneath.

I couldn't believe my eyes. Her black nylon hose went as far as her upper thigh where it was secured by a tight beige garter belt. There was quite a contrast between the dark stockings and her white protruding flesh that squeezed out from the edge of the belt. Fortunately for us her habit had stopped short of any panty sightings but the scene was enough to shock us all—especially Steven.

He dropped her limp arm to the floor and stepped back.

"Oh, my God! Oh shit! I'm scarred for life!" he called out as he rubbed his eyes and faked a gag.

Sister Claire struggled to help her fellow nun avoid any more embarrassment and adjusted the black fabric to cover her legs. Sister Bridgette's chin rested against her chest. But even in this precarious position Bugsy assumed her commanding role and demanded that we leave the choir loft.

"Go! Now!" she muttered weakly while waving an arm and pointing a finger over her head.

As we made our way down the stairs we squeezed passed two men on their way to help her. Once outside everyone enjoyed a good laugh as we recalled the sight of an exposed Sister Bridgette.

Meanwhile the bat continued to flutter around the front of the church causing an immediate evacuation. The bat in the belfry had certainly made its mark.

1969 A FLYING NUN
AND A MONK

As early as September I began to prepare for Halloween. One of my favorite holidays, it was right up there next to Christmas and I could barely contain my excitement. The idea of dressing as something or someone else for one day was intriguing and appealing to me. And surprisingly, the nuns at St. Timothy's let us celebrate the non-religious holiday at school. However, they had specific rules for costumes. They insisted we dress appropriately, preferably as religious characters—no devils or gruesome creatures would be allowed to wander the halls of St. Timothy's.

For weeks Ellen and I tossed around ideas about costumes. I had decided earlier in the fall what I intended to wear. Each Wednesday night my eyes were glued to the television as I watched the popular show, *The Flying Nun*, which starred Sally Field as Sister Bertrille. There was something magical and fun about her. She was not like any nun I'd ever seen at school. Sister Bertrille was always smiling and cheerful as she spoke with a gentle, sweet voice. The habit she wore was ivory instead of the gloomy black garments that the Sisters at school wore. Often times I wondered why they couldn't be more like Sister Bertrille.

For several weeks I worked on my costume gluing the cardboard pieces together to make the nun's unique winged headpiece. My mother was in heaven.

"Our own little nun! Wait till Grammy Fitzpatrick sees you!"

Both of them prayed daily that God heard their prayers. But unbeknownst to them I had already decided not to take that religious path. I knew by now that there was more to explore outside of the Sister world.

When Ellen saw my creation she stared in amazement.

"You look just like Sister Bertrille!" she exclaimed, her mouth wide open.

On the day of our Halloween celebration Sister Bridgette prepared a festive table at the front of the classroom to hold all of the homemade treats donated by parents. Brownies, popcorn balls, whoopee pies and chocolate chip cookies covered the entire surface. Sister's desk had been cleared of papers and pencils and now held an enormous bowl of penny candy consisting of red wax lips, jaw breakers, root beer barrels and tart candy necklaces, all graciously donated by the local JJ Newberry's.

After lunch my friends and I went to the girls' lavatory to change into our costumes. There were several Blessed Mothers and a few St Theresa's. Ellen wore a white silk robe of her mother's and pinned large chiffon wings to the shoulders. With a silver halo made of pipe cleaners and tin foil encircling her head of copper curls she was transformed into a beautiful angel.

Boys dressed up as priests and monks with a few St. Josephs and several St. Francis of Assisi's. Even Pope Paul VI was attending. With the party underway, noise and chatter from other class parties could be heard throughout the halls.

"Class! Class! Please line up it's time for the parade."

Sister Bridgette clapped her hands to get everyone's attention.

"Be sure to take a paper sack with you to collect your goodies."

As we waited in line Steven began his antics.

"Hey, what do you think of Bugsy's costume? She makes a wicked penguin!"

He and the boys roared with laughter.

"Is that what you're trying to be Muldoon?"

His words were hurtful, but I tried to ignore him, remembering that I was dressed as a good nun.

"Hey everybody! Mulldoon's turning into a crow!"

I heard the boys chuckling as we headed into the hall.

We paraded from classroom to classroom showing off our costumes. As we passed each teacher's desk we treated ourselves to a piece of candy and put it in our bag.

Excitement and laughter filled the halls of St. Timothy's, which didn't happen very often. For once the nuns were relaxed and allowed us to have some fun. Many students recognized my costume from the popular TV show and said how they loved it. The nuns even thought it quite special.

When we returned to our classroom Sister Bridgette announced the costume contest and said there were special prizes to be won. Each of us took a slip of paper and wrote the name of the person with the best costume—for both the boys and the girls. After inserting them into the shoe box on Sister's desk, we waited anxiously as she began to count the votes. The room was silent as Bugsy slowly drew the names and read them out loud.

"Ellen. Maureen. Ellen. Ellen."

My friend and I stood side by side as we patiently waited for the results.

"What could the prize be?" I whispered. "I hope it's something cool!"

"Maybe it's the latest Monkees record!"

Sister smacked her lips as she finished a cookie then made her announcement.

"Maureen, you are the winner of the best costume for the girls"

Everyone graciously applauded as I went to the front of the classroom to receive my prize.

It wasn't a Monkees record.

Hoping for something special, I opened the envelope and took out a wallet sized laminated picture of the Pope. That was it, a stinking holy card. Thinking there may be something else I looked deeper into the envelope. It was empty.

"Thank you Sister," I muttered.

Then it was the boys' turn.

"Michael. Steven. Steven."

Sister managed another bite of a treat as she continued to read the boys' names.

"It looks like Steven O'Hara is the winner of the boys."

Steven grinned from ear-to-ear as he went to the front of the classroom. He snatched the envelope from Sister and tore the envelope open. I watched with a grin as he turned it upside and began to shake it, as though something else was hidden inside.

Kids began to laugh.

"That's it? A Goddamn holy card? What kind of joke is this?" he muttered to me.

Thankfully, Sister didn't hear his remarks as she was helping herself to another whoopee pie.

The two of us made quite a pair. I, the nun, was the perfect match for Steven the monk. He wore an oversized brown wool robe and a large wooden cross hung from a leather string around his neck. His hair was completely covered with a rubber mask resembling a man's bald head.

Sister stood inches away as she looked down at us with a sinister smile. The lenses in her gray glasses magnified her drooping eyes and the edges of her bucked teeth overlapped her thick bottom lip. A crumb of chocolate cake dangled from the corner of her mouth. Bugsy's face, already pinched and wrinkled in the tight head piece, was flushed and her cheeks were puffed out like those of a squirrel accumulating nuts for the winter. She stood with her hands clasped against her protruding belly as the sunlight reflected against her white collar, emphasizing several straggly chin hairs.

She was no Sister Bertrille.

"Well, well. Looks like the two of you know what you'd like to be when you grow up!"

Neither of us answered.

"Is that right, Miss Mulldoon? Or should I say…Sister Maureeeeeeen?"

Sister's enormous teeth protruded further over her bottom lip as the corners of her mouth lifted like a Cheshire cat.

"Um…aaaah… I don't think so Sister" were the only words I could muster.

"Oh, we could train you to become a great nun! Your family would be awfully prouuuud! And of course, Jesus would love it too."

Bugsy never took her eyes off her protégé' and I felt my cheeks burn as she laid on the guilt.

"Yes Sister"

Winning was turning out to be no fun at all.

"And what about you?"

She turned to Steven and leaned in.

"Will you become Father Steven O'Hara?"

Steven tried to deflect her approach but much to my surprise he exclaimed, "Oh, yes, Sister!"

I flashed him a disgusted look. I knew there was no way he would or could EVER become a priest! But Sister was sucked in by his lie and flashed him a toothy smile. I knew O'Hara was just being funny and appeasing the nun. Moving closer to him she responded, "Well, perhaps you WOULD make a fine priest! It might be exactly what you need. Your parents would be prouuuud."

"Thank you, Sister!"

He tried unsuccessfully to scoot past the nun. Since I wasn't fooled by Steven's antics I decided to push the issue further.

"Sister, perhaps Steven should speak with Father Murphy."

Steven shot me a disgusted look.

"Well, perhaps he should! I'll have to talk to Father about that! Okay, you two enjoy your prizes and join the others."

With that, Sister Bridgette waddled over to her desk and snagged yet another Halloween treat. Steven was on my heels as I headed to the back of the classroom.

He tapped my unique headpiece and said, "Nice wings."

I kept going.

"What's the matter, Maureen? You don't want to be a crow? Looks like you're one already!"

Steven leaned forward and whispered in my ear. "Caw, caw, caw!"

That was it. I spun around to confront him.

"Shut up, O'Hara! You're such a liar. Everyone knows you would never, ever become a priest."

I glared at the boy with disgust.

"Arrgh! You stupid, bald headed monk!"

I lifted my chin to the air and continued to the back of the room. But Steven wasn't finished with me.

"Maureen Mulldoon went to the moon! Maureen Mulldoon you're a Goddamn goon! Ha, ha, ha! You and your red hair and cheeks!"

He said it loud enough that his friends heard it and began to laugh. But for once I was not going to let him have the last word. I was furious as I quickly spun around to face him which caused my Flying Nun headpiece to tilt to one side. We stood nose to nose.

"Oh yeah? Listen you little shit! Why don't you bring your bag of marbles tomorrow, huh? Then we'll see who's a goon!"

Steven's laughter subsided. We both knew how many times I embarrassed him at the game. And I knew it was one way I could get under my tormenter's skin. It seemed to work.

He gulped before he responded.

"Oh, Mulldoon, you're still a big ugly goon. Take your stupid marbles and go to hell."

"Chicken shit!" I snarled.

When I returned to my group of friends I could hear the boys snickering and laughing.

Steven Daniel O'Hara was relentless. It was embarrassing and I had had enough of him.

But little did I know how much of him I would have to endure.

1969 LETTERS TO HOME

I n the spring of 1969 a quiet young nun arrived at St. Timothy's to replace our teacher, Sister Mary Patricia. We had grown to like Sister Patricia, who had taken over our classroom, allowing Sister Bridgette to fulfill her duties as principal.

But then Sister Patricia disappeared.

It was on a Monday morning when we were told our teacher would not be returning to school. Bugsy said the nun had taken a personal leave—reasons not disclosed. But we heard the rumors, mostly from our parents. The gossip mill speculated that Sister Patricia had been having a heated affair with the handsome associate pastor, Father Edward Moore. Father had a gregarious personality and greeted everyone with his easy going way and twinkling green eyes. It was obvious how much he admired Sister Patricia for the extra effort she put toward church activities. The two had become a team, arranging various charity events that resulted in substantial financial contributions to the parish.

But parishioners loved to talk. Women from the Ladies Guild, Grammy Fitzpatrick included, observed the two at church functions and began to whisper each time they saw the nun and priest together. The topic became the main focus at our family dinner table.

"Well, well, well! Those two are a disgrace to the parish!"

"Laughing and smiling, they are! The devil has certainly worked his spell on them!"

Before long, word got out that Sister Mary Patricia had transferred to a school in Vermont. The rumor mill gained momentum and speculations of a baby began to surface. Everyone at school was buzzing with the news.

"Yes, I'm telling you...Sister Patricia did it with Father Moore!"

Father Moore, in the mean time, was immediately transferred to a parish some 60 miles away, which only fueled the gossip. Months passed and not another word was said about Sister Patricia. The nuns refused to speak of her, especially to students. Not long after the scandalous nun and priest departed Sister Mary Alice joined the staff of St. Timothy's. A petite woman, very delicate in size, Sister had thin lips and black framed glasses that hung precariously on the tip of her pointed little nose. She didn't look more than twenty years old. In fact, some students thought she could have been Sister Bridgette's daughter, that's if nuns had children. But thankfully, she was nothing like Bugsy.

Sister Alice was quiet and soft spoken in the classroom and it didn't take us long to figure out she had limited teaching experience. That explained why, from Sister

Alice's first day at St. Timothy's, she was observed by Sister Bridgette. It was unnerving to have the older nun, perched in the back of the classroom, watching our every move as she wrote furiously in her notebook.

Each morning, Sister Alice cheerfully greeted us as she entered the room.

"Good morning class! Good morning Sister Bridgette."

Even though she acknowledged her superior, her attempts were unsuccessful in breaking through the icy response she received each day.

"Good morning Sister Alice," replied a somber Sister Bridgette as she concentrated on her open notebook.

During class I could feel Bugsy's ever watchful eyes boring down on each of us as she examined our every move. She stayed in our classroom for approximately two hours before she quietly exited the room.

Once she was gone there was a definite change in the classroom, almost a physical relief. We were able to pass a note or whisper a joke to a friend. All of us were more relaxed, but none more so than Sister Alice. The visible tension disappeared from her face and she smiled even more. The nun never uttered an unkind word to any of us, even if someone tested her patience.

On a day when Steven threw spitballs across the aisle that landed on Janie's head Sister Alice kept her composure. She called both students to the front and made Steven apologize to Janie. The nun used positive words and actions rather than physical punishment. And, amazingly, it worked.

After six weeks of observation Sister Alice began to question Bugsy's motives. As we were taking a math quiz one day the room was quiet and I could hear the nuns whispering.

"Sister Bridgette, may I speak with you, please?"

"Yes, Sister, what is it?"

"Ah, yes, Sister. I was wondering if, perhaps, it was time for me to teach on my own without...."

"Sister Alice, reeealllly! Do youuuuu think you're ready to handle a classroom full of sixth graders?," she hissed. "I will determine when you are gooood and ready to be on your own."

"But Sister...."

"Sister Alice! Youuu are my protégé here at St. Timothy's. I will determine when the time is right. Now continue with your class."

Sister Alice mumbled, "Yes, Sister".

But on the following Friday afternoon something changed in Sister Alice. After finishing a period of mathematic equations we closed our books and put them in our desks. The next subject should have been our religion lesson but Sister Alice quietly went to a corner of the room. I was curious as she lifted the lid of a huge wooden record player. I'd never noticed that in our classroom before and wondered what the nun had up her sleeve. There was still thirty five minutes left until the final bell. I wanted so badly to turn around and see Bugsy's reaction.

Our class watched in silence as she placed a record album on the turntable and gently set down the needle.

Sister Alice turned up the volume. The classroom filled with the enchanting voice of Julie Andrews.

"The hiilllls are allliiiive, with the sound of muuuuuuusiiic!"

With her back to us Sister Alice hummed and swayed to the song. Then she went from desk to desk and handed out sheets of paper with the lyrics. Ellen sent me a quizzical look and I shrugged my shoulders in response. We didn't know what was happening. We'd already had our music class for the week.

My eyes followed Sister Alice as she went around the room. With a slight grin she handed a paper to Sister Bridgette, who snatched it from her hand. Sister Alice's cheeks were flushed as she spoke to the intimidating nun.

"Please join in, Sister."

Bugsy, however, would not be made a fool. She quickly grabbed her things and stormed out of the classroom, never saying a word.

As soon as she left, our class joined Sister Alice and sang along to the tunes from the *Sound of Music*.

The following Monday, in the middle of a spelling quiz the fire alarm rang and our class lined up to go outside. Everyone, that is, except Steven, who lingered behind.

"What are you doing? Get in line," I directed.

I became suspicious as I knew Steven enjoyed fire drills since they forced us to go outside and were a welcome break from the classroom.

Sister Alice quickly turned out the lights and led the class out to the corridor. Just as I approached the hall I glanced behind me to find Steven leaning over Sister's desk. He was snooping for the answer sheet! I watched as he grabbed a folded piece of paper from her desk and began to read.

"Holy shit," he muttered.

I lingered in the doorway with one eye watching out in the hall, ready to run.

"Is that the answer sheet?" I whispered.

"Oh, it's way better than that!"

He was grinning from ear to ear.

"Apparently Sister Alice REALLY hates Sister Bridgette! Oh, man, this is good, this is wicked GOOD!"

By now every class was heading down the back stairs. The two of us were alone in the classroom.

I couldn't resist and snatched the paper out of his hands. It was a letter written from Sister Alice to her parents. The young nun was venting her feelings about Sister Bridgette and her teaching experience at St. Timothy's. It was not a flattering letter.

Before I could do anything to stop him Steven grabbed the letter and his devious mind went on high alert. My heart pounded as I watched him sprint down the corridor. He paused outside of Sister Bridgette's office then tiptoed in. Finding myself drawn to his escapade, I acted as his lookout, making sure there were no nuns in sight. I held my breath as he tossed the letter that landed precisely in the middle of Sister Bridgette's desk.

"Oh my God, Steven!"

"Let's get outta here," he whispered breathlessly.

Instead of joining our class outside Steven quickly scooted into the boy's lavatory. I ran as fast as I could down the hall, to the flight of stairs and breathed a sigh of relief when I met up with my class. Thankfully, everyone was chatting and no one noticed that I had lagged behind. Minutes later we returned back upstairs.

Sister Bridgette stood staunchly out in the hall, monitoring us as we returned. Just as I approached my classroom, Steven sauntered out of the lavatory.

"Mr. O'Hara! What were you doing inside?" Sister Bridgette marched over to him.

"Sorry, Sister! When you got to go, you got to go!"

He shrugged his shoulders and quickly walked away, avoiding any more conversation with the ill tempered nun.

And Sister Mary Alice...within one week she was replaced. Everyone was sad to hear of the friendly nun's departure. Her absence meant Bugsy would be teaching us once again.

Guilt set in. I knew that wasn't our intention.

Disappointed students whispered and wondered. No one understood why Sister Alice would ever leave. Bugsy offered no explanation. But two of us knew exactly what happened.

Me and O'Hara the Scara.

1969 BLESS ME FATHER

The Sisters of the Blessed Sacrament said confession was a ritual that cleansed our souls and made restitution with God. By confessing, we were able to wipe away the indiscretions, lies and bad things we might have done or even thought about doing. All the black marks on our souls disappeared, were washed away after a visit to the confessional. It should have been a good thing, but I found the ritual to be a harrowing experience.

One day a month, the nuns ushered us to church to receive Catholic sacrament number two—Penance. The first sacrament of Baptism had been received within weeks of our birth. Baptism prevented anyone that died from spending eternity in limbo. And no one wanted to be in limbo. It was a place where your soul waited and depended on others to pray for you before you were allowed in heaven. And you never knew how long that might take.

Confession prepared us for the third big sacrament, First Holy Communion. Church law stated before anyone received Holy Communion at mass they had to confess their sins to God.

Sister said the parish priest was our direct connection to Jesus.

"It's like talking to God" the nuns reassured us.

We were told that we were born with sin but as hard as I tried I couldn't remember doing anything wrong. We learned the difference between mortal and venial sins; the bad and really horrible sins.

"Children, you are all sinners! Therefore you must, must, MUST go to confession as often as you can."

Sister Bridgette drilled the scary notion into our heads during every religion class. I listened wide-eyed, afraid of what might happen if I *didn't* go to confession. I imagined all of the venial sins that I must have carried around in my soul. After all, I had bad thoughts about Bugsy all the time. And I daydreamed about kissing David Cassidy and Davy Jones. And when Steven O'Hara teased me...well, I found myself wishing bad things on him.

The monthly ritual began early in the day when Sister instructed us to contemplate and think about our sins to confess.

"Class! Quiet please!" Sister Bridgette announced.

"Bow your heads and think about your sins. We will be heading over to church shortly."

For the next several minutes I squeezed my eyes shut and thought about everything I'd done. I cussed at my brothers and called them names, even though I caught them reading my diary. The day before, I wished that Steven would drop dead. And as usual I had hateful thoughts about Bugsy.

Then I also prayed that I would remember my list. It seemed there were many times when my mind went blank in the confessional. As Father patiently waited for me I quickly made up something to confess, feeling the guilt of yet another lie. The whole experience was stressful.

"Class, line up at the front!"

Before leaving school, Sister verified that each girl had something to cover their heads. None of us normally carried our mantillas with us, except for Janie, so tissues and bobby pins were handed out. The thin wisps of paper blew in the wind as we walked to church. As we followed other classes out the front entrance and across the driveway I tried to ignore the passersby on the sidewalk who teased us.

"Look at those poor little cat-lick kids!"

An old man with missing teeth remarked to his friend as the two of them shook their heads and roared with laughter. Steven wasn't taking it.

"Take a goddamn picture it'll last longer!" Steven retorted as he quickened his step.

Once in church I touched my fingertip to the bowl of holy water and made the sign of the cross. Sister led us down the middle aisle. The church always felt mystical to me. Beautiful chandeliers cast a soft glow against the polished oak pews and the scent of incense lingered from an earlier mass.

Sister Bridgette gestured to us to take our seats in the pews adjacent to the confessionals. I genuflected to the altar then sat down. The confessional booths were located on both sides of the church. An ornate wooden door was flanked by two narrow entrances, each covered by a burgundy velvet curtain. The priest always sat behind the door although I never saw him go in or out of the room.

My stomach fluttered. No matter how many times I went to confession I was anxious. Sister prayed as she knelt in the row directly behind us. After a minute or so she took her position at the end of the pew where she motioned to us one at a time and watched as we entered a confessional.

I waited patiently for my turn. Steven swung his legs casually under his seat and looked around the church. As usual he was fidgety and provoking the boy next to him. I was relieved he was sitting in the row in front of me.

Everyone knew the average time for confession was approximately 3 to 4 minutes. And a simple penance should only take five minutes. Penance was one or several prayers, Our Father, Hail Mary, or Glory Be and was determined by the severity and number of sins confessed. Saying them acknowledged wrongdoing and made absolution with God. The prayers were said outside the confessional in a pew at the front of the church. It became a game to watch and monitor each student as they left the confessional. We surmised the longer the penance, the worse the sins were, or at least the number of sins.

Steven was growing impatient.

"What the hell is taking so long?"

He stood and looked around.

"Somebody must have a lot of sins!"

"SSSHHHHH!"

Afraid that Bugsy would hear him students told him to be quiet. I could hear mumbling from the priest as he said his blessings.

"Maureen!"

Sister Bridgette whispered loudly. I folded my hands and went to the confessional. Pausing briefly just outside, I took a deep breath then pulled back the heavy curtain and stepped inside. The cubicle was tiny and completely dark. I reached out and felt the small shelf located just above the kneeler in the left corner. As I knelt down, I folded my hands on the shelf and bowed my head. My heart was pounding in my chest as I listened to Father Murphy give his absolution to another student.

I jumped when the narrow rectangular window suddenly slid open. Just seven inches by four inches it allowed a small amount of dim yellow light to be filtered through the decorative metal screen. I glanced up to see the side of Father Murphy's face as he sat inside the cramped room and I could smell the lingering scent of a freshly smoked cigarette. I cleared my throat and began.

"Bless me, Father, for I have sinned. It has been one month since my last confession."

I paused, as I tried to catch my breath.

"Go ahead."

Speaking very softly and slowly I began to recall the sins I had thought of earlier when suddenly my mind went blank. I panicked.

I fabricated something about missing mass and taking the Lord's name in vain then finished with "and I lied" as good measure for everything I had just told him.

"Is that all?" Father whispered.

"Yes Father."

The priest recited prayers of absolution, forgiving me of my sins. He mumbled them so fast I had no idea what he was saying. Finally, I heard my penance.

"Say two Hail Mary's and two Our Fathers."

"Yes, Father."

"Now please recite the Act of Contrition."

"Oh, my God, I am heartily sorry for having offended thee...."

Pleased that I remembered the entire prayer I breathed a sigh of relief when I finished.

"In the name of the Father, the Son and the Holy Ghost, Amen," I whispered as Father blessed me with the sign of the cross. Feeling cleansed, I bowed my head and proceeded to the front to say my penance. As I passed the second confessional I heard Steven's loud voice.

"Bless me Father, for I have sinned."

In the front row I knelt beside Francis who finished his penance and was now busy creasing the pages in several of the hymnals. I closed my eyes and began to pray.

"How many did you get?" Francis leaned forward and tapped me on the shoulder.

"Not as many as you!" I whispered.

As I waited for everyone to finish I watched Steven saunter to the front with his thumbs in his front pockets.

He knelt down and said a prayer in record time. We all knew it couldn't possibly have been his entire penance. When he sat down he noticed everyone watching him.

"What? What the hell are you looking at me for? Mind your own goddamn business!"

Horrified, kids gasped at his cussing like that right after leaving the confessional—and in the front pew no less.

"I'm telling Sister!" Janie stood and whispered fiercely to Steven.

Unfazed, he looked her directly in the eye and said, "You do that McMack, and you'll have me to face at recess!"

The girl sat down and never said another word. We all knew O'Hara the Scara did not make idle threats. By the time our two classes were finished students were shifting in their seats, whispering and giggling. Sister Bridgette and Sister Alexander worked the crowd like two keystone cops. Just when one section was quieted down another began chatting and making noise.

When the nuns led the parade of our newly cleansed souls back to school Steven was directly behind me and continually stepped on the heel of my shoe causing it to slip off.

"Your souls are pure now, children!! Let's keep it that way!" Sister Bridgette proudly exclaimed.

It didn't take long.

By the time we were back in the classroom I already had bad thoughts about Steven.

And just like that, I had new black marks on my soul.

1969 REPORT CARD TIME

E very morning at breakfast as I got ready for school, my mother reminded me to raise my hand in class.

"Make sure ya raise yer hand!" she declared. "The Sisters will love ya for it!"

I nodded my head in agreement even though I knew I would never be raising my hand unless I definitely knew the answer. It was mortifying to be put on the spot by one of the nuns, especially if I was uncertain of an answer. My parents, however, thought it was important to show some interest in class and prove to the nuns I was trying my best.

My mother kept close tabs on my homework and when it was time for report cards she was sure to ask about the upcoming grades.

"So, what do ya think, Maureen? Will it be all A's this time?"

I tried to appease her.

"I don't know, Ma. I've been trying my best."

If I had any doubts I certainly was not going to tell her. I'd rather take my chances and pray that my grades met her expectations. There was no doubt I would find out long before she did, even before I got to read the report card myself.

Discovering what grades would be given was not only apprehensive for me but my classmates as well. Along with that, we had to wonder about the comments Sister Elizabeth might write on the report card concerning our behavior and attention in class. Sister was notorious for writing colorful personal commentary regarding class participation and tardiness on the back of each report card.

And then there was the matter of Father Philip Murphy.

For decades it remained customary for the parish priest to hand out each student's report card.

And facing Father Murphy was like facing God.

On report card day our class was exceptionally quiet as we waited for Father Murphy's arrival. I had knots in my stomach as I watched Sister Elizabeth at her desk obsessively stacking the brown envelopes. I glanced around the room and saw apprehensive looks on others. No one looked forward to Father Murphy's admonitions. We never knew what the priest might say.

There was a gentle knock on the door before he entered the classroom. The priest shuffled in as he scuffed his heels across the polished floor. We immediately stood to greet him.

"Goooood afternooooon, Faaaather Murphy" we chanted in unison.

Sister Elizabeth glided over to meet the priest and bowed slightly. He gave her a curt nod as she followed him to the front of the classroom. Sister stood off to one side, holding the mound of report cards.

"Good morning, children, good morning." Father said in his gravelly smoker's voice.

"Sit down, sit down, now."

He waved his hand impatiently signaling us to return to our seats. You could hear a pin drop in the classroom as we watched and waited for the process to begin. As instructed, we kept our hands folded on top of our desks. No whispering or talking was allowed as we gave the priest our undivided attention and respect.

Father Philip Murphy was probably only 60 years old but his demeanor made me think he was 100. His thick, greasy salt and pepper hair was slicked back revealing a shiny protruding forehead. He wore black framed Clark Kent glasses with extremely thick lenses that magnified his bloodshot eyes making him look like Mr. Magoo. Dressed in slacks and an ankle length cassock he was completely encased in black except for the small square section of white in the middle of his collar. A small bronze crucifix with a black chain hung from his neck. Although short in stature, Father's presence was threatening as he stood hunched over with his hands clasped behind his back. All eyes stared back at him as he slowly scanned our class. I prayed his eyes would not meet mine.

"I expect that each of you did your very best this marking period."

No one answered.

He paused to cough and I could hear rumbling coming from his lungs.

"Sister Mary Elizabeth has been working you very hard, I'm sure. But getting good grades is imperative! Imperative, I tell you!"

Again, the disturbing cough.

"Yes, Father" several of us mumbled in response.

I glanced over at Ellen and both of us rolled our eyes. I clenched my hands and took a deep breath, wishing the whole process to be over. Father gestured to Sister Elizabeth that he was ready to begin.

"Now, let's see how everyone did."

He took the first report card.

"Steven O'Hara."

Steven rose from his desk and dramatically hiked up his pants for a laugh before proceeding to the front. It was no surprise that even this formality didn't faze him. Steven stood directly in front of Father Murphy and looked up at the priest who opened the report card and began to read aloud.

"Let's see. You have a C in Math. That's alright. B in Spelling, that's good, good. A C+ in English. Well, Steven, it looks as though you've been paying attention. But, wait a minute. You have a D in Religion? Religion? How can that be?"

He stared at Steven, who slowly shrugged his shoulders. Then he glanced behind him to be sure his audience was paying attention before he replied, "I don't know, Father. Why?"

The priest was not amused and leaned in closer to Steven.

"You're a real smart aleck, aren't you, Mr. O'Hara? How about trying to bring this grade up next time. Quit your joking and apply yourself!"

Steven leaned back and waved his hand quickly in front of him as though attempting to escape the smell escaping from Father's mouth.

"Yes, Father."

As Father handed him his report card he puffed out his cheeks as he held his breath then bowed slightly. When he returned to his desk he let out an exaggerated sigh and again waved his hand in front of his face as a distinct warning to the rest of us. One by one students were called to the front to receive Father's commentary and criticisms.

"Maureen Mulldoon."

I smoothed my skirt, walked to the front and looked up at Father Murphy. When he began to read my report card I immediately recognized the stale scent of cigarettes wafting from the priest. The strong vapor of tobacco was mixed with something else...I couldn't determine what it was, but I desperately wanted to take a step back. I held my breath.

"Okay, what do we have here? You have a D in Math. Oh, Maureen, that's not good. Not good at all. You are going to have to work on that! And a B in Spelling. Well, it looks as though you find that more interesting. You have an A in English as well. Good, very good. And a B in Religion. Very good. Well, my dear, you had better work harder in Math."

He leaned closer.

I looked at his eyeballs that were enormous behind the thick lenses. My gaze moved down to his mouth. Father's crooked horse teeth were smoke stained and surrounded by thin purple lips. White spittle had begun to accumulate in the corners of his mouth. I wondered how long it would be before the substance would fly off. I couldn't hold my breath any longer and audibly released it before speaking.

"Yes, Father."

I barely heard what he said as I never took my eyes off his mouth. The white foam was getting thicker.

"You need to keep trying, Maureen. I would hate to see you stay back in fifth grade because of your math. Don't be lazy, now. Do all of the work and study hard. If you apply yourself you'll see this grade improve in no time."

He handed me the report card.

"Yes, Father."

I wanted to run. I didn't want to be so close when that nasty saliva let loose. I bowed slightly and quickly retreated to my desk anxious to escape the science project between his lips.

The priest repeated the process until he summoned the last student, Francis O'Neal, to the front. Everyone waited in anticipation as Francis was the other class clown. Every week he and Steven were always getting into trouble in one way or another with the nuns. Francis arrived late to school most mornings with his clip-on tie dangling from his collar and his shirttail always out. His mass of curly brown hair was always a mess and most days his shoelaces were untied as well. Francis was the youngest of ten children and not bashful in the least bit. Since first grade there wasn't a week that went by that Francis wasn't sent to the principal's office for talking excessively or laughing too much. Around school he was known for his imitation of the nuns. Francis constantly disrupted the class with a funny outburst or comment and the nuns were exasperated with him. Even when his spanking was heard over the school intercom system, Francis continued his antics. I thought he was pretty cute. He had big blue eyes and the deepest dimples in his freckled cheeks. I didn't care that he looked sloppy when he came to school because he was fun to be around.

"Francis O'Neal."

Father Murphy repeated a little louder as he scanned the classroom and wrinkled his nose to keep his glasses on his face. Everyone giggled as Francis looked around the room. Then he said innocently, "Oh, me?"

He jumped clumsily from his seat and sauntered to the front. Francis stood in front of the priest with his thumbs in his pockets. As usual his shirt tail was out and one shoe was untied. I was curious to hear what Father would have to say about his report card. As Father Murphy began to read the grades aloud Francis began doodling on the floor with the toe of his shoe.

"Well, let's see Mr. O'Neal. What have we here? You have a C in Math. That's not bad. You received a D in English. D? Oh, that's not good. An F in Spelling? Obviously you are heading for disaster Mr. O'Neal! Oh, that is not good. Not good at all. Why do you think you have an F in Spelling? You know how to spell, I'm sure!"

The priest leaned in closer to Francis, his face just inches away. The boy scuffed his foot while still looking at the floor and shrugged his shoulders.

"Beats me" he answered.

"Francis!" Sister Elizabeth called out as she took a step toward him.

Without looking over Father Murphy put his hand in the air, stopping her from saying anything else.

"Beats me!? Beats me? Now, do you think that's an appropriate answer, young man? You can do better than a D in English! If you apply yourself you will see your grade go up!"

Father paused, waiting for a response, and adjusted his glasses further on his nose.

"I think perhaps you'd better stay after school and get some extra help with your spelling, Mr. O'Neal. Otherwise you are going to end up repeating this grade!"

Francis remained silent.

Father Murphy tried to remain calm, but the report card began to shake in his trembling hands. It was obvious he was losing his patience.

"What do you think your parents are going to say about this?"

He shook the report card in front of the boy.

"Beats me."

This time Francis glanced at the class behind him. A couple of girls giggled at Francis' antics and it was just the response he was looking for. The rest of us sat frozen. I knew he was pushing his limits. An agitated Sister Mary Elizabeth rubbed the tips of her fingers across her brow. There was no denying that Father Murphy was annoyed because his droopy cheeks were flushed bright crimson.

"Look here, Mr. O'Neal!"

With a snap he lifted Francis' chin and peered into the boy's eyes. Francis glared back at Father Murphy. But when he saw the accumulated foam in each corner of the priest's mouth, his eyes grew wide. Each time the man moved his lips the white spittle stretched like two wet rubber bands.

"Well, Mr. O'Neal. It appears to me that you think this is all a joke. Well, sir, IT IS NOT A JOKE!"

By now, the bubbly foam was visible from the back of the room. At any given moment the moist substance would let go. The class watched anxiously as Francis carefully took one step back never taking his eyes off the priest's mouth. He had to hurry.

"Goddamned kid!" The priest muttered as he let go of Francis' chin.

Father Murphy had taken the Lord's name in vain!

"Yes, Father."

Francis knew he'd pushed his limits and hung his head.

"St. Timothy, pray for us!" Father exclaimed with his hands in the air. And just then a glob of foam flew from his mouth and landed on the front of Francis' oxford shirt. Father must have sensed it because he reached up and wiped the corners of his mouth with his thick fingers. And in an instant, with that same hand he handed Francis his report card. It all happened so quickly the boy took the card without thinking. Poor Francis! A moist spot had begun to penetrate his cotton shirt making it cling to his chest. He hurried back to his desk without taking his eyes off the dark wet circle that appeared on his report card. He clasped the card delicately between two fingers and dramatically held it in front of him as he went back to his seat. He wrinkled his nose and carefully dropped the envelope on his desk. Several kids giggled at his theatrics. I reached over and handed Francis a tissue.

"Thank you very much Father" Sister bowed to the priest. "Class, what do you say to Father Murphy?"

"Thaaaaank you Faaaaather Murrrrrrphy!" we chanted in musical unison.

Father blessed our class with the sign of the cross as he recited "In the name of the Father, and of the Son, and of the Holy Ghost, Amen."

"Aaaamen."

As Father Murphy shuffled out the door he said sternly to Sister Mary Elizabeth, "Good luck with this bunch, you're going to need it!"

Sister Mary Elizabeth wasted no time. As soon as the door was closed she headed straight to Francis' desk.

"Mr. O'Neal! Your behavior was deplorable! Stand up right now and go to the blackboard."

Her student showed no remorse. He'd had this punishment numerous times before. The only difference was he didn't know what he'd be writing. Francis flinched as Sister grabbed the top of his ear and led him to the front of the room. The boy winced as she continually twisted his ear.

The only time she let go was when she wrote on the board.

'I will show respect to Father Murphy at all times' was scrawled across the top. She handed Francis a piece of chalk then smacked him across the back of the head.

"Write this sentence fifty times, Francis. Perhaps it will sink into that thick skull of yours."

She rubbed her hands together to remove the chalk and calmly said, "Class, please take out your composition books."

For the next forty five minutes Sister Elizabeth taught us the basics of writing an essay while Francis wrote the sentence over and over again on the blackboard. He was still there when our class was dismissed that day.

I didn't see the art work until the following morning. In a corner of the blackboard was a caricature of Father

Murphy. The perfect depiction outlined his face, complete with glasses and bulging eyes. And in each corner of his mouth was a white ball of spittle.

If there was one subject Francis O'Neal excelled in, it was Art.

1969 THE SPEECH

My stomach churned at the thought of standing in front of my sixth grade class to read my current event. Public speaking was not something I excelled in and I swore Sister Bridgette knew that. She had suddenly decided it was time for our class to read our reports aloud instead of turning in a written paper. Good ole Bugsy just had to make things difficult.

Just after her announcement and as soon as the last bell rang, I gathered my books and hurried outside to meet up with Ellen. As we strolled up Church St towards Main I didn't waste any time to vent about Sister Bridgette.

"Bugsy is such an old witch!" I shouted. "I don't want to do that oral report tomorrow!"

"She's not just a witch, Maureen."

Ellen glanced over her shoulder to be sure no one else was around. "She's a downright bitch! But don't spaz out! Just prove her wrong. If you practice tonight you'll be fine!"

I brushed past my friend and marched into Woolworth's.

"I need candy!"

I was frustrated and as usual, felt something sweet would help me cope.

I really hoped that Ellen was right and that if I practiced my speech everything would be okay. I just hated being the center of attention. I could read aloud from my desk anytime, but the idea of standing alone, in front of everyone was just too much. Teachers said I mumbled but I didn't think I did. And I blushed so easily! It was aggravating because it happened for no apparent reason. But I had no way to control it. Of course Steven had a comment each time my face turned red.

"Wow, look! Look at your cheeks! Why are you turning red, Maureen?"

It only made things worse.

Once home I grabbed a Tab and found the newspaper then climbed the stairs to my room. After changing out of my school uniform I settled in to work on the report. Normally, I would have watched *Dark Shadows* after school but on this particular day I felt it was important to concentrate on the assignment.

I decided on an article about the new urban renewal project taking place in our city. It meant tearing down the entire Main Street and was talked about by everyone. I cut the story out of the newspaper and took out a sheet of lined paper. Being that I loved to write, it only took a few minutes to complete my own interpretation.

I stood in front of my maple dresser and looked into the mirror. When I read aloud I could be sure the narrative flowed smoothly. After the second reading I could feel my cheeks getting warm. When I caught my reflection I saw two blotches of pink slowly creeping on either side of my face.

"UUUGGHH, I hate that!"

It was an Irish trait I wished I could get rid of. While saying my prayers that night I asked my guardian angel for help while I gave my report.

Please don't let my face turn red, Amen.

The following morning I was up fifteen minutes early to prepare for school. I had butterflies in my stomach so I thought it best to skip breakfast. My white blouse and plaid jumper were neat and clean. In the bathroom I scrubbed my face and fussed with my unruly curly hair.

"Why did I get these stupid curls?" I muttered to my reflection. I wet my fingers in the sink and tried to smooth the stubborn waves. I finally gave up and headed outside to meet Ellen for our walk to school.

It wasn't until after lunch that Sister Bridgette began calling on students to do their reports. The wait had been pure torture. One by one I listened as students were called to the front of the class and proceeded to recite their written articles. With her grade book and pen in hand, Sister stood and observed from the back of the room. Occasionally she interrupted a student and questioned the grammar they used. She was a stickler for proper grammar.

"Excuuuuuse me, Mr. Hough! Since when do we end a sentence with a prepositional phrase? Hmmm? You should know better."

As Joseph Hough scrambled for an answer Sister made notes in her grade book.

"Take your seat Mr. Hough."

I watched as a dejected Joseph hung his head with shame as he returned to his desk.

"Maureen Mulldoon, you're next."

Finally. I just wanted it to be over. I reached down and pulled up my navy blue knee socks. Then I stood and smoothed my skirt.

"It's snowing down south!" Ellen whispered to me frantically.

I grabbed the waistband of my half slip and hiked it up. When Ellen gave me the A Okay sign I took a deep breath and tried to shake off the nerves which only made my mouth extremely dry. My upper lip stuck to my front teeth and I quickly gathered spit to moisten my mouth. As I took my place in front of Sister's desk and turned to face the class my eyes remained focused on the report in my shaking hands. I cleared my throat then slowly began to read the report just as I had practiced the night before. Within seconds Sister Bridgette rudely interrupted by shouting from the back of the room.

"Caaahhhn't hearrrrr youuuuuu!"

Please, Bugsy cut me some slack I thought as I glanced up briefly at the nun, cleared my throat and once again began my speech.

For the second time, I heard, even louder, "Caaahhhn't hear youuuuu, Miss Mulldooooon!"

Sister Bridgette's sing-song voice was laced with disgust. I could feel the heat on my cheeks and knew they had to be fiery red by now. My heart pounded as though it would leap out of my chest. Why did the old crow have to be so mean? At this point I was more angry than scared. It was completely silent in the room. The only thing I could hear was the ticking of the clock as the rest of the class sat in silence, watching and waiting for me to finish.

Once again I began my report, a little louder this time. Or so I thought.

"The new urban renewal committee is scheduled...."

"Maureen...Mary...Mulldoooooon! You need to speak up! I cannot hear youuuuuu!"

Exasperated, Sister Bridgette slammed her grade book down on the empty desk in front of her. The nun was not giving up.

"BEGIN AGAIN!"

My legs began to quiver and I felt clammy all over. The paper began to visibly shake in my trembling hands. My mind was fuzzy and I felt as though I were floating in a dream. What had only been a minute felt like an hour as I stood there. I swallowed hard and fought back the urge to cry. I cleared my throat once more and I gave it my all. When I spoke I even surprised myself. It was as though my voice were someone else's. In the next few moments I felt no fear. My voice was assertive and loud and I concentrated on the words written on my paper and plowed through the article. When I looked up, to my astonishment, Sister Bridgette was standing just two feet in front of me. I was so engrossed in delivering my report I hadn't even noticed her approaching. Her arms were crossed in front of her as they rested on her protruding belly and she glared at me through her cat's eye glasses. Her gray menacing eyes were magnified by dirty lenses and a sneer exposed her enormous yellow teeth. I was panic stricken and mesmerized by the frightening sight. What the hell do I do now? And why was she standing so close? Her expression revealed to me that she was really angry. My mind was racing, my heart pounded wildly and I began to feel slightly dizzy.

"Well Miss Mulldoon, you think you're pretty funny, do youuuuu? Hmm? Well, I think not!"

I could smell her stale breath. Was that onion or a day old cup of coffee?

"I will not be made a fool of young lady. You may take your ridiculously curly red hair AND your incompetent report and go SIT DOWN!"

As she swiftly raised her hand and pointed a crooked finger towards my desk I involuntarily flinched, afraid that Sister was about to strike. Just as I turned away I caught a glimpse of the dark mahogany rosary beads tied around Sister's thick waist. How ironic that she wore something so sacred. Perhaps she ought to use them.

"Miss Mulldooooooon, you can forget about EVER becoming a public speaker!"

That was it. In one swift instant my spirit was deflated. It would take me years to overcome her biting remarks. I managed a whisper.

"Yes, Sister."

"Take your seat Maureen. Just… take…your…. seat."

Sister repeated in a low voice. I felt unsteady and kept my eyes to the floor as I went back to my desk. I was mortified. My heart was pounding so hard I would have bet money that the entire class could hear it. And what the hell did my hair have to do with my report? Why did she have to embarrass me in front of the class?

As I passed Steven he covered his mouth with his hand and laughed as he silently pointed a finger at me. Suffer wicked, I mouthed to him.

I don't remember much else that happened for the remainder of that class. My mind was spinning as I thought about what Sister had done, how she made me feel.

I hated that nun. I didn't care if it was a sin. I hated her for the way she talked to me.

But most of all I hated her for filling me with shame and guilt.

1970 THE BIRD

Every October a local photographer was hired by the school to take individual student and class pictures. The gymnasium was converted to a makeshift studio and throughout picture day classes took their appointed turn to have their photos taken. At 1 pm my seventh grade class headed down to the gym.

Because of the shortage of nuns I was blessed, once again, to have Sister Bridgette as my teacher that year. Always a perfectionist, she insisted that we make ourselves presentable. The other girls and I fussed with our crisp white oxford blouses and pleated navy and green plaid skirts, which were to be no higher than our knees. Little did the nuns know that when they weren't looking we rolled the waistbands of our skirts over and over again to shorten them. Sure it made it a little bulky around our waists but doing so kept us with the latest mini fashion. We got away with it until one of the nuns noticed. Knee socks, ankle socks or tights were accepted but nylon hose on Catholic school girls was strictly forbidden.

The boys tucked in their light green oxford shirts and straightened the forest green clip-on ties embroidered with the school's initials—STS. If one of them forgot their tie there were plenty of paper ones available in the principal's office. No one knew who actually sat down and cut each of those out of green construction paper but I'm sure it was a punishment for someone.

Our class processed single file down several flights of stairs. One by one we announced our names to the photographer's assistant as we entered the gym. The bored woman handed us a mini plastic comb and an envelope for payment.

"Here's a comb. Please check your hair in the mirror."

The assistant's monotone statement was repeated over and over again. I grabbed the black comb and turned to look in the mirror that was set up at the far end of the table. It was no use. I didn't even bother to run the comb through my hair. I tossed the comb in the trash and hoped for the best. After individual shots were taken, the photographer arranged our class by height for the group picture. I really hoped to be standing next to my best friend, Ellen, but as luck would have it I was next to Steven. After looking around I decided I was better off next to the lesser of two evils. Sister Bridgette stood at the end of my row and I thanked God I didn't have to be photographed next to her.

"Hey Mulldoon, what's the matter with your face?! Jesus, it looks like you've been standing behind a screen door!"

The irritating boy poked me in the ribs. I flinched and instinctively swung a fist into his upper arm.

"Shut up Steven!" I said through clenched teeth. "Don't touch me again!"

"Did you forget to comb your hair this morning, Mulldoon?"

I felt my cheeks flush with embarrassment. He was such a jerk.

"By the way, you're flying low", I lied.

Steven scrambled to check his zipper.

Minutes later the photographer raised his hand before calling out, "One, two three, say CHEEEEESE!"

The school pictures arrived three weeks later and Sister Bridgette distributed the packages after lunch.

"Hoooolllly crap!" Ellen exclaimed as she examined the class photo. I glanced over to see what she was talking about.

"What's the matter?"

"Look at the class picture. Look!" Ellen whispered. "Hurry up!"

I pulled the photo out of the envelope and saw it, plain as day.

There was Steven, posing with a huge toothy grin, with his hand purposely positioned directly in front of him.

He was giving the camera the finger.

My mouth dropped open. Steven would be catching holy hell for sure! I looked around to see if anyone else had noticed. There would be no escaping this one.

"Steven is going to be in biiiiiggg troooo-ouble." I whispered to Ellen. We both began to laugh. One by one students began to whisper as they saw what Steven had done. Giggles riffled around the room.

"Steven's giving the bird!"

"Look what O'Hara did!"

When Steven saw the photograph he tossed his head back and proudly laughed along with his friends.

"How's that for balls?" he exclaimed.

That is, until he remembered Sister Bridgette. He glanced up at the nun sitting at her desk and began to fidget in his seat. I watched his excitement fade.

By now, Sister had seen the photo. All eyes were on Steven as we watched the scene unfold in the quiet room. O'Hara the Scara would have to work hard to charm his way out of this one. Unfortunately, he didn't stand a chance. The proof was in the picture.

Steven raised his hand and waved it wildly.

"Sister, Sister, may I go to the lavatory?"

He blurted out his question before the nun had a chance to call on him, breaking one of her strict rules. But he was too late.

With the ticking of the clock the only noise in the room, I watched Sister Bridgette clench the photo tightly in her hands. Her anger was clearly visible.

"MR. O'HARA!"

Bugsy slammed both of her hands on her desk and dropped the picture. A stack of papers toppled over and landed on the floor. She slowly pushed herself up and pushed her heavy chair, causing it to scrape loudly across the wood floor.

I jumped in my seat. I'd never seen Bugsy like that before. The expression on her face was dark and more sinister than ever. The nun's bloodshot eyes were glazed behind her glasses. And her bushy white eyebrows were tightly creased together, rippling the skin on her forehead. Sister Bridgette's bucked teeth pressed firmly into her lower lip and her puffy cheeks began to flush crimson. From my seat in the back of the classroom I could see her chest heaving. Pausing for a moment she glared directly down the aisle at O'Hara the Scara.

Steven attempted to avoid her stare. He gulped as though he had something stuck in his throat. For once he was at a loss for words. He began to wiggle in his seat, his legs jumping back and forth like he really did have to go to the bathroom. The boy's freckled face drained of color. I'd ever seen him look so scared.

Sister Bridgette moved slowly and deliberately as she made her way to her victim's desk, never taking her eyes off him. Her wide hips bumped into one desk and then the other. The bulky fabric of her habit rustled as she squeezed herself down the aisle. She knocked a textbook off Francis O'Neal's desk and it landed on the floor with a heavy THUD startling all of us. But no one dare make a move so the book stayed there. It was amazing that she was able to maneuver up the narrow aisle. She was unfazed. As Sister passed their desk each student lowered their head, not wanting to be in her line of vision or make eye contact.

Jesus, Mary and Joseph, I thought as I looked at her hand. Sister had a tight grip on a wooden ruler.

I wasn't the only one to see it.

Steven was becoming desperate as he spotted her weapon. He looked around at his friends for support but no one could look him in the eye. Suddenly he began to blurt out one lie after another.

"Sister, I don't know how that happened! I don't remember doing that, Sister! I'm sorry, Sister. I'm really sorry!"

But the lies didn't matter. It was as though she couldn't hear him. Sister stopped and hovered over her prey. Any attempts at Steven resolving the issue were futile.

"Mr. O'HAR-AAA"

Everyone jumped in their seats. Sister Bridgette's quivering voice had gone up at least one octave. The furious nun's chest heaved up and down as she inhaled and exhaled deeply. Her nostrils flared and her lips were pursed. Sister glared at the top of Steven's head. The boy didn't move a muscle.

"HANDS ON YOUR DESK!" Sister Bridgette bellowed.

The ruler was now clearly visible to everyone as Sister held it in front of her. The class nervously looked on and one girl gasped loudly then made the sign of the cross. We'd all heard of this punishment being given, but none of us had actually witnessed it. Most times the hitting of the knuckles was broadcasted over the loud speaker from the principal's office.

I stared at the intimidating form of Sister Bridgette, just several feet in front of me. She appeared larger than life. Her swollen protruding belly pressed against Steven's shoulder as she shouted at Steven again.

"Mr. O'HAARRRAAAA!"

Steven hesitated, then slowly took one of his shaking hands from his lap. He placed his palm on the edge of his desk.

"I ….said….BOTH…hands …on…your….desk!"

Sister leaned forward, her face coming very close to Steven's own. He crinkled his nose in disgust and reached up with his other hand holding his nose in defiance as a last attempt for a laugh. But no one was laughing. I slowly shook my head, the boy was just asking for trouble.

"NOW!"

Steven jumped in his seat. His comedy act was not going to save him now. He jolted upright and stretched out his arms, placing his hands flat on the maple desk. Then he held his breath and focused his gaze on his fingertips. I watched in horror as Sister slowly raised her arm and pointed the ruler to the sky, looking as though she were holding a sword and prepared to strike. Her billowy black sleeve slipped down to her armpit as she readied herself for attack. I stared at the nun's pale flabby arm. It had obviously never seen the sun and looked like a squishy old marshmallow. Sister Bridgette tightly clutched her rosary beads with her left hand.

"YOU ARE THE DEVIL'S CHILD!"

WHACK!!

The sharp crack of the ruler shattered the silence as it met with Steven's knuckles. Ellen jumped and put a finger in each ear. I could only stare. Jesus! Bugsy was off her rocker!

"ARE YOU SORRY FOR YOUR SIN, MR. O'HARA?"

Steven was obviously in excruciating pain.

"Y-y-yes, Sister."

He squeezed his eyes shut as she raised her arm once more then took a deep breath and held it, waiting for Sister's next hit.

WHACK!

Again the ruler smacked hard on Steven's hands. His knuckles glowed bright red. I held my breath and watched intently thinking I might see blood any second. The sound was horrible. Ellen couldn't watch what was happening and closed her eyes. Steven bit his bottom lip that was beginning to tremble. Even though he brought it upon himself I began to feel sorry for him.

"Do you realize what you've done, Mr. O'Hara? You have RUINED the picture for the entire class! Ruined!" Sister Bridgette declared loudly. Her blood shot eyes were wild.

"Answer meeeee, Mr. O'Hara."

Her voice was deep and low and she spoke through clenched teeth.

"Y-y-yes Sister." Steven muttered as he choked back tears.

She raised the ruler once more then slammed it on Steven's hands a third time.

WHACK!!

"Yooooouuuuu aaaaahhhrrre a DISGRACE to this class," she shouted.

Her arms were now tightly folded in front of her. With the rapid breathing the large wooden cross around her neck heaved up and down. She continued to glare at Steven while he rubbed his hands together.

"I will see to it that you meet with Father Muuuuurrrphy first thing tomorrow morning for confession! But for now, young man, you are going to the office! Bring this disgusting photograph with yoooouuu. I will meet you there to contact your parents."

Steven gathered his pictures and other belongings. His jaw was clenched as he tried to suppress the pain. I wondered if the bones were broken as it looked as though he couldn't move his fingers. I knew he would not want anyone to see him cry.

"Oooooooh nooooo young man! You are NOT taking your things. You will be coming back here after school. Just take the picture and start walking."

She thrust her arm toward the door. Everyone watched as Steven stood up from his desk. With his eyes cast down he hurried out of the classroom. I had never seen him show so much emotion, but I had a feeling I knew why. Steven would be getting punished at home as well. Everyone knew his father liked to use the belt. None of us moved. Sister's anger was still visible and no one wanted to endure her wrath. She wasn't afraid to lash her nasty mood onto others and it could last for hours.

"Class put the pictures away and take out your multiplication tables. We are going to have a drill."

Her voice trembled as she carefully made her way back to her desk, sat down and placed the ruler in the top drawer. The nun's cheeks were still flushed a deep red, her eyebrows still furrowed, and her lips were pursed together very tightly.

Ellen and I exchanged glances but neither of us dared to speak. With our multiplication table on our desks we waited quietly, observing Sister Bridgette.

Sitting very still at her desk the nun began clenching and unclenching her fists. Her eyes were lowered and she never looked up at us. With trembling hands she took out a tissue and wiped her nose.

Could it be that she was actually sorry for what she had just done? If she had a conscience she would have been.

"I will return shortly but for now study for your quiz." Sister's voice quivered.

My eyes followed her out of the room then gazed up at the large detailed crucifix hanging on the classroom wall just above Bugsy's desk.

Jesus had seen it all. Would He still love Steven with another major black mark on his soul?

And what about Sister Bridgette?

I said a silent prayer that God would allow O'Hara the Scara's soul into Heaven.

1970 FORGET THE TWIRL!!

The Sisters of the Blessed Sacrament enjoyed a good musical and jumped at any opportunity to produce a variety show. Immediately after Halloween, the nuns began organizing and planning for the annual Christmas performance. The holiday pageant was by far the most spectacular show of the year. It was presented twice, once in the afternoon for students and staff and then again at night for parents and the community. Preparations for the event took months. Sister Claire put hundreds of hours into compiling the holiday music, lyrics and dance numbers. She collaborated with several of the other nuns and together they scripted an entertaining tale featuring toy soldiers, dolls and of course the finale, which depicted the blessed family and baby Jesus in the manger.

Each year it was a challenge for the nuns as they determined who would be portraying Blessed Mother and St. Joseph. Even though they were not speaking roles, they were considered the stars of the show. The nuns said their decision was based solely on class behavior. But none of us were fooled.

Janie McMack had played the part of the Blessed Mother for two years straight. As beautiful as Janie was, Sister Claire made it known to Sister Bridgette that it was time for someone else to take over.

For years I wanted that role. I knew I'd never get to crown Mary in the May procession, as that part always went to the tallest girl in class. My only hope was that of the Blessed Mother in the Christmas pageant.

But it was not to be. Surprisingly, the nuns did not select Janie, but Barbie Holland, and I was resigned to portraying a doll. The show's theme that year was that of a child's toys coming alive in the middle of the night. Dolls and teddy bears would dance together to the musical score, *Sugar Plum Dance* from the *Nutcracker*. The boys were divided—some played the part of toy soldiers and would dance the *Nutcracker March* while others took on the roles of teddy bears.

On the first day of rehearsal Sister Bridgette paired us up for the big dance number.

I prayed and prayed to be paired with Francis. He was cute and so damn funny. No one could make me laugh like Francis O'Neal. One by one Bugsy pulled a boy from the line up and placed him next to one of the girls, sizing them up to be sure they could dance cohesively. It didn't take me long to see the outcome. Before I knew it I was standing next to Steven.

"Hey, Mulldoon aren't you the lucky one today!!"

Steven chastised me as soon as he took his spot. He nudged my arm and gave me a wink.

"This is gonna be reeeeeeeeal good!"

I could feel my cheeks tingling and flush so I turned my back to him with my arms defiantly folded. I looked at Ellen and rolled my eyes.

Steven leaned in close behind me and whispered, "Mulldoon, don't be such a goddamned goon!"

I was tempted to ask Sister Bridgette if I could change partners but I knew she'd never change her mind.

"They're all yours, Sister Claire!"

Bugsy stormed off showing no further interest in our rehearsal. Sister Claire came forward and one by one, placed us in the starting position on stage. Sister was authoritative without being demeaning therefore we were willing to comply.

"Okay, children, you MUST remember your places. It is very crucial for each dance number!"

The nun rushed over to the side of the stage and turned on the decrepit Magnavox record player. She carefully placed the needle onto the album and turned up the volume. Sister crossed her fingers and prayed the record didn't skip then returned to the front of the stage. With the music blaring we watched her demonstrate the proper dance position using Francis and Ellen as examples.

Francis was ever the jokester. Each time Ellen reached for his hands he flung them behind his back or over his head.

"Francis! Stop it!!" Ellen whispered fiercely. But Sister Claire had the patience of a saint. She spoke softly to

Francis and asked that he be the lead in the group, giving him responsibility. Francis calmed down and decided to cooperate. He and Ellen slowly demonstrated the entire dance number.

"Ladies, just let the boy lead. Boys, be gentlemen," she announced as she lifted her habit two inches off the floor and began to demonstrate the dance steps.

"Step to the side, step to the side. Then one, two, three, one, two, three!"

We watched Sister glide across the stage on the tips of her nun shoes while swaying and humming along with the record.

"Look at the ugly crow's feet!!" laughed Steven. I reached over and flicked him on the arm. Sister Claire looked as beautiful as any nun could while she danced in front of us.

"Continue this process until the second stanza. When I give you the signal you will repeat the steps in reverse. Now, let's begin!"

She scurried over to the console, lifted the needle and announced over her shoulder, "Places, everyone!!"

I turned to face Steven and reluctantly took hold of his hands, which were disgusting. His palms felt soft but were clammy and warm. He sticky fingers held my hand gently. After each number I quickly let go and wiped my palms against my plaid skirt. I thought about wearing a pair gloves at the next rehearsal.

I don't know how Sister Claire stayed so calm. None of us were very good dancers. After a frustrating hour of practice Sister announced she would be adding another element to the dance routine.

"Boys, I want you to hold the right hand of your partner high over your head. Then girls I want you to stand on your toes and twirl around twice, very slowly, before dropping your partner's hand. Both of you are to turn and face the front of the stage. Girls, you will then curtsy and boys you will take a bow. Now, let's try it!"

I took hold of Steven's sweaty hands and began the dance steps. At the end of the number Steven raised my hand over his head but we didn't finish the sequence. Just when it was time for me to spin around Steven dropped his arm and said, "Forget the twirl". I wondered if he was aware of the same smell I had inhaled when he lifted his arm. Could it be that he was embarrassed? He was quick to turn away so I didn't have time to argue. For the next thirty minutes we practiced the same dance sequence over and over, each ending the same way.

"Forget the twirl."

Several times I whispered to him and said we needed to practice but it was of no use. Steven would stop, fold his arms defiantly and wait for the music to finish. I glanced over to Sister Claire, hoping we wouldn't get into trouble. I pondered whether or not to tell her what was happening. But I didn't want to embarrass Steven or give him any more reason to torment me.

For the next several weeks Steven did the same thing. Not once did we finish the entire dance number and I wondered how it would turn out the night of the show.

Mrs. Holland, Chubby's mother, my mother and Mrs. Callahan volunteered to sew the girls' costumes. Over several weeks they made beautiful life-sized baby doll dresses complete with pinafores.

Excitement was in the air on opening night. After assisting us into our outfits my mother applied makeup to each of us. Rosy red cheeks, pink lips and dramatically painted on eyelashes completed the look of an exquisite baby doll. My hair was pulled up into two small curly ponytails and tied with brightly colored ribbons. I was amazed when I looked into the bathroom mirror. I looked very pretty dressed up as a doll and I thought once again how much I would have liked Francis as my dance partner.

Our group of dolls and teddy bears waited anxiously just out in the corridor, adjacent to the stage, while the toy soldiers performed to the *Nutcracker March*. I looked over at Steven who was dressed in a furry brown costume complete with mittens that resembled large paws. Super! No sweaty hands! I smiled in relief. He caught my eye and I waited for one of his smart ass comments. But all he said was, "Hey......Mulldoon."

Then I saw a grin. I glanced around. Was he really smiling at me?

At that moment Sister Bridgette approached our group and through clenched teeth began to whisper loudly.

"Hurry! Get into your positions! It's almost time for you to go on. Quickly, quickly!!"

We scurried about with our partners and silently waited to go onstage. The audience applauded as the group of toy soldiers exited the stage.

Sister Claire came and silently motioned for us to take our places. We filed in behind the stage curtain and took our designated spots. The lights were low and there was a buzz of excitement in the air. I felt butterflies in the pit of my stomach as the familiar music began.

As we began the sequence of steps across the floor I wondered about the twirl. I glanced up at Steven who had the strangest look on his face. What was wrong with him?

Then, as if in slow motion, Steven stepped closer to me, took my hand and raised it high above his head. Without notice, I followed along as he twirled me once, then twice.

With each twirl the tips of our noses came dangerously close. I caught him staring at me which caused a flutter in my belly. The music ended as the audience began to applaud and we turned to face the crowd.

I didn't notice until we turned to leave the stage. As we took our bows, our hands we still tightly clasped together.

That night I knew everything had changed with me and O'Hara the Scara.

1971 THE JIG IS UP

The month of February was filled with rehearsals for the much anticipated St. Patrick's Day variety show. Every day after lunch, classes were led down to the gymnasium for rehearsal. Sister Mary Claire was once again put in charge of the program but ultimately Sister Bridgette had the last word. Sister Claire desperately wanted to change the opening solo. For several years Cathleen Black had opened the show, much to the dismay of Sister Claire.

The thirteen year old girl loved to dance. The problem was she wasn't very good. But year after year she was inevitably given the opportunity by Sister Bridgette to perform a solo jig. Rumor had it that the decision was based on the substantial financial contribution made by Cathleen's parents to the parish.

Doing so allowed her parents to attend rehearsals whenever they wanted to watch their daughter practice.

Unfortunately for Sister Claire, Bugsy had once again promised the spot to Cathleen. Her only consolation was it would be Cathleen's last since she would be graduating in the spring.

Throughout her elementary school years Cathleen stayed committed to her dance lessons. Her instructor agreed to attend rehearsals to help the girl. But even he was dismayed as he cautiously told Sister Bridgette that she was the chubbiest ballerina he'd ever seen. Inevitably, her leaps ended with a loud and heavy THUD. Graceful she was not. As Cathleen practiced and moved across the stage, both Sister Claire and Sister Bridgette hovered over the large record player. Cathleen's cumbersome landing would unfailingly cause the record to skip. The nuns were ready to scoop up the arm of the needle and place it back into position.

In addition to Cathleen, each year Ellen and I were instructed to perform a double Irish jig in the St. Patrick's Day show. We hoped and prayed that Bugsy would choose someone else, but it was not to be. The two of us were the same height with fiery red hair and a face full of freckles. Sister Bridgette was convinced that the two of us epitomized the typical Irish lass. Her excuse to us was that Norman Rockwell couldn't have conjured up a more fitting picture.

But we hated performing.

At the age of thirteen I somehow summoned up the courage to ask Sister if we could have a different part in the show.

I should have known.

"Miss Mulldoon! How daaaarrreee youuuu even ask such a thing!" she roared.

I sulked back to my seat. Ellen and I grimaced at one another and shrugged our shoulders. It was no use.

As with every other year when performance day approached I began to feel anxious. Neither of us had any formal training and even with years of doing the jig we were very uncomfortable with the audience's eyes watching our every step. Just days before the show Sister Bridgette gave us costumes that had been donated by a parent, themselves an Irish dancer some twenty years before. The outfits consisted of two identical traditional Celtic dresses and used black leather dance shoes.

"These should fit just fine, girls."

The knee length dresses were faded but tolerable with billowy green skirts adorned with hundreds of small white embroidered shamrocks. The shoes however were another story. They were much too big for either of us to wear comfortably, never mind dance. The black leather was extremely scuffed and worn with the front tips curled up. Two long tattered green ribbons dangled from each shoe. Ellen and I looked at one another. Sister had to be joking. Feeling brave, Ellen took a deep breath and cautiously approached the nun.

"Excuse me, Sister. May we wear our own shoes for the dance? These are much too big and…."

Bugsy interrupted and exclaimed, "Youuuu ungrateful thing, yooouuu."

She pointed a finger at Ellen and continued, "These are authentic Irish dancing shoes donated in good faith! Yooooouuuu most certainly willlll wear them."

With a huff she turned on one heel and left us with the decrepit footwear. I crisscrossed the long tattered ribbons around my ankles and tied them as tight as I could in hopes of keeping the oversized shoes from slipping off.

"Jesus H Christ! I'm sorry, but these are wicked nasty!" Ellen spat. "I'd like to see the old penguin wear them, never mind try to dance."

During practice I clenched my toes tightly to keep the slippers from falling off and by the end of one session both feet were cramped up. Ellen came up with the idea of filling the toe area with tissues to keep them from flopping around but it didn't help much. We crossed our fingers that no one would notice on show day.

Finally on Wednesday, March 17, 1971 the variety show opened with Cathleen dancing to an Irish classic, *The Kesh Jig*. Sister Bridgette scurried back and forth behind the stage. With a crooked finger to her lips she shushed us over and over again even though everyone was completely silent.

I huddled with Ellen and several others as we watched Cathleen struggle through the first number. It was painful to watch. Outfitted with black tights and dance slippers she wore a snug, unflattering, sparkling green leotard. The costume outlined every ripple and dimple in her chubby form. As she grunted and groaned making the twists and turns, Cathleen's shoulder length strawberry blonde hair swung wildly as she danced. Strands of it clung to her flushed face. As the end of her number came to a close Sister Claire hurried to the Magnavox. Cathleen pirouetted over to the side of the stage to prepare for the final jump. With one heavy leap she landed.

THUD!

The music began to stutter. Sister Claire quickly picked up the needle while Cathleen continued to dance. Without any music in the background, laughter began to ripple through the audience. When Sister replaced the needle back onto the album it was not in sync with Cathleen's routine. She was two steps ahead and way out of rhythm. However, Cathleen was in her own little world.

Sister Bridgette was beside herself as she paced and muttered under her breath while making the sign of the cross. Ellen and I stayed out of her way.

"Looks like Cathleen's had way too many frappes at Weeks Dairy Bar!"

Steven whispered loudly. "Someone ought to buy her a bigger leotard!"

Several of the boys began to laugh.

"SSHHH!"

I turned and looked at him with disgust. I felt sorry for poor Cathleen. With relief, the music ended and Cathleen took her bows, oblivious to the audience's laughter.

The eighth grade boys then performed their rendition of *Harrigan*.

"Miss Mulldoon and Miss Callahan! Get ready! You're next."

Sister Bridgette barked as she briskly waddled over to us. Ellen and I looked at one another and sighed. Our only consolation was that this would be our last Irish jig to perform—ever. After Sister Claire gave the signal we walked slowly to the front of the stage and took our positions. A light applause rose from the audience. I was so nervous that I couldn't even look out to find my family. Instead I stared straight ahead out the window at the far wall of the gym. My right hand was curved over my head and the left one placed on my hip as I waited for the music to begin. The familiar tune started and we began. I'd heard *The Irish Washer Woman* enough times to know each beat by heart.

With just minutes left I felt my right shoe begin to loosen. I needed to finish this one last jig. I curled my toes tightly as my feet continued to sweep quickly back and forth, back and forth. I shifted from side to side in time with the music. With just one more pirouette left I'd be done.

Then I felt it. My shoe slowly slipped off and was dangling by the ribbon tied tightly around my lower calf. I glanced over at Ellen who looked down at my foot. It was a mistake to look at one another. The two of us burst out laughing as we made the final spin with my worn out dance shoe flopping on the stage. I was laughing so hard I couldn't see anything through the tears. But I kept going. Ellen, on the other hand, was so out of control she couldn't finish the number. She was doubled over, holding her sides that throbbed from the incessant laughter. When the music stopped I turned to my friend and we hugged one another in relief. The audience was expressionless. Silence was broken when all of a sudden I saw my Dad who stood and slowly began to clap his hands. Then Ellen's Dad stood. One by one the entire audience began to applaud. Ellen and I held each other's hand as we curtsied and took several bows.

As I headed off stage dragging my shoe behind me my eyes met Steven's. I felt my cheeks get hot as he stopped directly in front of me and looked down at my feet and whispered, "Don't you know how to tie your shoes, Mulldoon?"

"You are such a dink!" I sneered and turned away. The only thing I could hear behind me was Steven's sarcastic laugh that ended with a snort.

I turned and gave him a look. That boy was really getting under my skin. But when I turned back around I came face to face with Sister Bridgette. She stood sternly with her hands on her hips, leaned forward and looked directly into my eyes.

"Yooouuuuu my dear, have some explaining tooooo doooo!"

"Um Sister, it was um, an acci-"

"No excuses! No excuses, Miss Mulldooooon."

Then she reached up, snatched my left ear and gave it a sharp tug. My eyes filled with tears. She finally let go and took one step back, all the while glaring at me.

I didn't know what to do. I needed to put my shoe back on and get ready to go back onstage for the final number. The nun shook her head and turned away. I quickly tried to shake off the hateful feeling from Sister. While the stage curtain was closed, several nuns assembled the backdrop for the finale. We got into our positions and readied ourselves for the last song of the evening.

It was my favorite Irish tune to sing. When the curtains opened we belted out a fabulous rendition of *When Irish Eyes Are Smiling*. I looked out into the audience and found my Dad. His huge smile said it all. He gave me the A-O-K sign and I felt much better.

At that precise moment I forgot all about the messed up dance number, Sister Bridgette and even Steven O'Hara.

1971 GOPHER

My eighth grade year was my last at St. Timothy's. For seven years I had gone through school with the same group of classmates and we'd come to know each other like brothers and sisters. We were from all walks of life but together we learned the traditions of the Catholic faith and expanded our education through lessons taught by the Sisters of the Blessed Sacrament. Some lessons we learned were not just from the nuns, some we learned from each other.

The summer before I entered eighth grade I had minor surgery. During my adolescent years a small mole had grown smack dab in the middle of my neck. The doctors called it a pigment but by the time I turned thirteen the thing was bigger than a pencil eraser. It was very noticeable and just one more thing to deplete my self confidence.

The previous year, in seventh grade, Steven had begun to tease me about the mole. I don't know why he felt it necessary to embarrass me like he did.

"Hey Mulldoon, you stinky goon, what's that on your neck?"

It didn't matter if we were heading to church, in line for lunch or out at recess, the boy was relentless.

I tried to talk to my parents about him.

"Ah, sounds like he has a crush!" was all that my father would say.

Ellen tried to comfort me with the same reasoning.

"I think he really likes you. That's why he does it."

But it was no comfort to me. Over the years Steven had been boisterous in his comments about my cheeks turning red and my curly hair. I was able to dismiss his negative attention until I approached my teen years and became more sensitive. His words stung even more. And when I tried to lash back my emotions got in the way.

"Shut up, Steven!" I would begin to retort, but the tears would well and I would back down and turn away.

It wasn't fair. The nuns heard what he said but they never intervened.

There was one particular incident in February of seventh grade that truly put a damper on my self confidence. We were preparing speeches to be done in front of the class. The presentation was on desired career choices. Mine was interior design.

I found it exciting to put together a room with a variety of colors and different types of furniture. There were many afternoons Ellen and I transformed my tiny bedroom. As we rearranged my bed and dresser my mother would stand at the bottom of the stairs and yell, "What's going on up there?"

Even in the cramped space we were able to arrange the bed, dresser and desk to give my room a whole new look.

I prepared my speech with cut out pictures of colorful rooms in different categories of design, doing my research at the public library. I learned about the required education and the excellent income that could be earned and I was excited to present my topic.

On the day of presentations Sister Bridgette announced her instructions.

"Please give your attention to the speaker. There's to be no talking."

She stood at the front of the classroom, just behind the wooden podium.

"And presenters! Please take your time. Speak slowly so that we understand you. And speak up so I can hear you from the back. Okay, let's get started."

I felt the flutter in my stomach as memories came flooding back. Even after all the years of oral reports and current events I was not used to speaking in front of the class. I took deep breaths and tried to stay calm because I didn't want my cheeks to get red. I had prepared that morning by waking early, making sure my uniform was neat and clean. And I even tried something new with my hair. The night before I used some pink hair tape I purchased at Woolworth's with babysitting money. It was the latest product to tame the curls and it had been easy to sleep on. When I went to bed my entire head was crisscrossed with pink stripes in hopes of flattening and securing the waves on my head. And it worked. With a little hairspray I was able to control the stubborn tendrils. I felt confident that morning. I just wanted to be able to recite my speech without having to read the entire thing directly off the index cards, which Bugsy frowned upon.

First to go was Francis O'Neal. He presented the career of an airline pilot. I visualized him in his uniform and thought he'd look very handsome.

Then there was Janie. Of course her aspirations were to become an actress, fitting for her because she loved drama.

Two more students went on to present their reports before stopping for lunch. Down in the cafeteria I sat across from Ellen.

"I just want this to be over!" I said quietly.

"You'll be fine. It seems to go by pretty quick. But I know what you mean. It's a relief to have it done."

The lunch room was noisy with clanging trays, chatter and laughter.

Out of the blue I heard a familiar voice.

"Mulldooooon, you stupid goon. What's that on your neck?"

A shiver went up my spine. I said a silent prayer, please God, not now. Please make him stop.

"Just ignore him." Ellen leaned across the table and whispered to me.

"Hey, it's ground hog day and you look just like the gopher!"

I continued to eat my grilled cheese sandwich as an attempt to ignore his remark.

"Hey gopher!"

His laugh was boisterous and loud.

"Gopher, gopher, gopher!"

All of his friends around him began to laugh. I felt my cheeks getting hot. I knew if this kept up I would be beet red when I had to deliver my report.

"I need to go to the lavatory."

I quickly got up from my seat and proceeded to ask permission from Sister Oliver, who was the cafeteria monitor that day. She must have seen the pained expression on my face because she did not hesitate to say yes.

When everyone returned from lunch Sister Bridgette began to call on students.

"Gopher!" I heard a hard whisper coming from behind me, then snickering. I could hear Francis, who sat beside me, stifling a chuckle. I was hurt that he fell for Steven's rude behavior.

When Sister Bridgette called my name I hesitated and looked down at my stack of index cards.

I wasn't sure I could muster up the courage.

I slowly got up from my desk but instead of going to the front I went to Sister who was sitting at a desk in the back of the room. The room was silent as everyone watched me.

"Sister, I'm not prepared." I said softly. I was shaking. I didn't know what her reaction would be. But miraculously her response was quite gentle.

"You're not prepared? Do you need more time, Maureen?"

"Yes, please, Sister." I felt the tears come quickly.

She must have sensed why because she told me to stay after school so we could talk. I was shocked but agreed to her request.

Then she whispered softly, "Go to the lavatory and rinse your face."

I stayed at my desk while the other students left school that day. Ellen asked what was wrong. I explained that Sister had asked me to stay, I was okay and she didn't have to wait.

Once everyone left and the classroom was empty Sister approached me.

"Maureen, why didn't you do your report today?"

I tried to explain but once I began it sounded so childish. I stopped talking afraid that I would cry and make Sister angry. But somehow the nun understood.

Apparently she must have witnessed Steven's behavior towards me.

"It's Mr. O'Hara, isn't it?"

"Yes, Sister."

"I tell you what. You may do your report right now if you'd like."

I couldn't believe my ears. Was this the same Bugsy who liked to ridicule me?

"Now?"

"Yes, go on. Go to the podium."

Just then Mr. Lachant, the janitor, entered the room. Sister motioned for him to continue his cleaning.

I stood at the podium and looked up at the American flag hanging in the back corner. I cleared my throat and began. My speech was flawless. Mr. Lachant wiped the floors back and forth with his mop but he never looked up.

Sister Bridgette came to the front when I finished.

"That was excellent, Maureen, excellent."

My jaw dropped and I breathed a sigh of relief. She said I could go home so I gathered my books and exited as fast as I could before she changed her mind.

I think I was in shock. Something had changed with Sister Bridgette. I wasn't sure what but it was a good change. I received an A for my report and I never did another presentation in front of a class again until I was in high school.

The summer before eighth grade my parents decided it was time to have the mole on my neck removed. I was quite nervous about it but if it would stop Steven, or anyone else, from teasing me than I knew it had to be done. The simple procedure was done right in the doctor's office leaving a pink two inch scar that replaced the ugly brown pigment.

When classes began just after Labor Day in 1970 I was excited to return. It was an important school year as our eighth grade class would be the last to graduate from St. Timothy's.

As I walked up the front steps of school I felt a nudge.

"Hey, Mulldoon! What's happening Gopher?"

I let out a deep sigh. Not again, please God. I ignored him and continued upstairs to my classroom.

He wasn't deterred. He pushed by other students to keep pace with me as I hurried down the corridor. Students and nuns were everywhere. The younger children looked scared as they tried to find their classroom. Others like me who'd been there a lot of years, strode confidently to their room. Just as I stepped in the doorway Steven scooted in sideways, right beside me. We were face to face.

"So, Mull..." He stopped short. It was at that moment he saw the scar on my neck.

His expression was priceless. I'd never known Steven to be at a loss for words.

"Hmph!" I smirked and continued to my desk.

Later in the morning as my class descended down the stairs to the cafeteria Steven maneuvered his way to walk beside me.

"Hey, Mulldoon, I mean Maureen."

Something had changed. Perhaps it was the fact that I didn't have the mole anymore. But it felt like it was more than that. Throughout the morning Steven never once teased me. No whispers of Gopher, no teasing about my hair. Something was different.

Several times while I ate my lunch with Ellen and the other girls I caught Steven watching me. When our eyes met he suddenly looked away. I wondered what was wrong with him.

The following Sunday I attended the 9:00 am mass with my mother, sister and two brothers. As the organist began to play, the priest and altar boys processed onto the altar.

I couldn't believe my eyes. There was O'Hara the Scara dressed in a red cassock topped with a short crisp white cotton covering. Steven was an altar boy! It was a miracle. Was this the same boy who scared a nun half to death with a frog!? Or who teased and called me names?

As Mass went on I couldn't concentrate on any of the prayers because my eyes were focused on Steven.

His demeanor was completely different than at school. He was solemn as he carefully brought the cruets of wine and water to Father Murphy during the Eucharist. When Mass ended I lingered by the back entrance. I wanted to see if perhaps his parents or siblings would be there.

Steven came around the corner and smiled when he saw me.

"Hey Mulldoon, I mean Maureen!"

Chills ran up my spine. But I wasn't sure why. I couldn't be certain but I think Steven had finally grown up. He was finally being nice to me.

No more Mulldoon the goon. No more teasing about my cheeks. But most importantly, no more gopher.

Eighth grade was starting off in the right direction.

1971 CHANGES

In the fall of my eighth grade year the Sisters of the Blessed Sacrament changed their habits—literally.

The higher ups with the religious order had finally listened and obliged the newly recruited nuns. To change with the times the board reviewed and passed bylaws that adjusted the requirements of the clothing the religious women wore. After decades of carrying the weight of the heavy, black, muslin dresses; long black veils and tight headpieces, the Sisters now had a choice. The older more conservative nuns refused to change and continued with what they knew. Sister Bridgette, Sister Alexander and Sister Dympna chose to wear the traditional nun garb. Sister Oliver and Sister Cornelius were a little more daring as they chose to wear a shorter version with the hem just below their knees. We could actually see their legs! And their veils were much shorter with a simple white band that surrounded their forehead showcasing a wisp of bangs. We could actually see hair! The lightweight veils flowed down and stopped at their shoulders. They wore the rosaries around their waists but the beads were smaller, less cumbersome.

"Oh my gosh! Did you see Sister's legs?"

"Sister Cornelius has red hair!!"

The excitement at school was contagious. None of us expected to see that much of our teachers exposed.

But the biggest change of all was Sister Claire and Sister Louise. They were the youngest nuns at St. Timothy's. Sister Louise had been hired in October and was taking over as my eighth grade teacher. Their dress choice was a dramatic one because they wore civilian clothing—actual skirts and blouses and simple loafers. The pieces were simple in structure, no floral or bright colors, with the length of the skirt just below the knee. Instead of rosary beads around the waist they wore simple gold crosses around their necks. And to really separate them from the other Sisters they did not wear veils at all. They actually showcased a full head of hair. Of course all of them continued the tradition of wearing the plain slim gold band on their left ring finger, symbolizing their relationship with Jesus and the church.

Like most students, I spent a lot of my life at St. Timothy's wondering what was underneath those headpieces and veils. We talked about it at recess.

On days when the wind blew furiously we hoped that a gust would pick up their veil in hopes the mystery would be revealed.

"Do you think they're bald?"

"I bet they shave their heads."

At last we had some answers. Sister Louise had wavy brown hair that was just long enough to be pulled low to the nape of her neck and secured with a brown barrette.

Sister Claire had beautiful shiny black hair. She wore it in a short bob that framed her face which gave her the look of a foreigner as though she hailed from Europe. Her dark locks contrasted with her bright blue eyes making her stunning. Her eyebrows were shaped perfectly. And again I just had to wonder to myself why someone so beautiful and sweet would want to devote her life as a nun.

Other changes had also taken place. Boys were beginning to show signs of puberty. Francis O'Neal had a dark shadow on his upper lip and one of the boys definitely needed some deodorant. Steven looked taller having grown a couple of inches since last June. And there was a dramatic change with the girls as well. Most of us had purchased bras, which had been a subject of crisis in my house over the summer.

"Mom, I need to get rid of these childish t-shirts! Pleaaaasse can you buy me a bra?"

After weeks of pleading she reluctantly agreed that her little girl was growing up. She took a trip to JJ Newberry's department store where, I believe, she bought me the most uncomfortable brassiere on the rack. It was constructed of stiff white cotton with absolutely no stretch to the fabric. The bra's rigid straps dug into my shoulders and it felt extremely tight around my waist. The nearly empty cups were unnaturally pointed. A lot of other female bodily changes were taking place within me as well.

Over the summer I convinced my mother to stop the haircuts and allow my hair to grow. By fall it was longer which helped with the tussle of curls. On some nights, Ellen and I rolled each other's hair in new pink spongy curlers. With our barrage of supplies consisting of curlers, tape, hairspray and silver hair clips I managed to keep my locks under control.

The entire class was showing signs of maturity. Girls were flirting with boys. And the boys were even more obnoxious. Janie McMack was not as snobby as when she was younger and at the beginning of October she delivered party invitations to each member of our class, including the boys.

"Here you go! I hope you can make it!" she said sweetly as she handed out the envelopes.

I tore the envelope open hoping it was a costume party.

You are cordially invited to a Halloween party.
Please dress in your scariest or funniest costume!
Prizes to be given. Games to be played. Snacks to be
provided.
Saturday October 30 @ 6:30 pm

I was excited. My first teenage boy/girl party! Even though Janie was the host I anticipated many others to attend so I wouldn't have to socialize with her as much. I looked forward to dressing up in a costume since it would be the first year I would not be allowed to go trick-ortreating in our neighborhood. My mother had informed me that since I was a teenager I could not dress up and instead I would be taking my siblings to the neighbors to collect their candy.

Eighth grade was also the year of our final sacrament in school. Starting in the fall Sister Louise's religion class taught us the importance of Confirmation. It signified a time when we would be anointed with blessed oil or chrism and receive the blessing of the Holy Spirit, administered to us by the bishop.

"This is a very important rite of passage" Sister Louise explained. "it will unite you even more so with Christ. It's a blessed sacrament indeed."

We studied for weeks. We were taught receiving this sacrament strengthened our relationship with the Catholic Church and we would be committing our lives to living the Catholic faith. A part of the process included choosing a sponsor, usually a family member, to guide you through the process during mass. I chose my Aunt Mary who was mother's younger sister and just fourteen years older than me. We were extremely close so I wasn't surprised that she eagerly accepted the honored request. The next step was to choose a Confirmation name, usually that of a saint or in remembrance of a family member. Although it would be the only time we would use the name, the nuns suggested we give it some thought. They wanted the Confirmation ceremony to be special.

"I'm picking Sgt. Schulz, like the TV show *Hogan's Heroes*!" Steven joked.

Sister didn't think his comment very funny so she went to her desk and pulled out a small prayer book.

"I think you will find an appropriate one in here" she said as she handed it to Steven who reluctantly began to browse the pages.

"Hey, here's one. St. Innocent! Haha, yep, that's me!"

Sister returned to his desk and flicked him on the back of the head.

"Please, take this serious, Mr. O'Hara!"

In the end Steven chose St. James and I chose Christina in honor of my great grandmother.

Sister Louise emphasized the importance of good behavior during the special Confirmation mass.

The diocese office directed Bishop Philip Joseph to perform the mass in October. For weeks we went over the prayers and rituals. The practice paid off. Our class was exceptionally well behaved. Even Steven wore a solemn expression as he approached the bishop and recited the appropriate responses while his uncle stood behind as his sponsor. I felt grown up as I stood before Bishop Philip with my Aunt Mary's hand resting on my shoulder then she gave it a squeeze before returning to her seat. When mass was over our class joined our families in the gym for refreshments provided by the ladies guild.

Aside from the important sacrament, my mind constantly thought about the upcoming party at Janie's. I decided to wear a gypsy costume. It was one way to glam it up by wearing loads of costume jewelry and makeup.

Excitement could be felt in the classroom as just about everybody in class would be attending.

Several girls were standing in a circle at recess when Janie approached.

"I don't care what your costume is," Janie declared with her nose in the air "but none of you had better dress as Twiggy. I'm the only one that will look that cute for the boys!"

Typical Janie. After she walked away we began to speculate what sort of outfit she'd be wearing that night. Twiggy was an extremely skinny model known for her tight miniskirts and high patent leather boots. Her pictures were in all the latest magazines.

Ellen rolled her eyes as Janie skipped away. She didn't have to worry about me as I would not be allowed out of the house wearing a mini skirt.

My costume for the party consisted of a long flowery skirt and an oversized silk blouse borrowed from my mother. Several beaded necklaces, a colorful scarf around my head and large clip-on hoop earrings completed the look. Ellen looked especially cute in her black cat costume. At 6:15 we strolled to Janie's who lived just a few blocks away. As we got closer we met other students who were also attending. There was a hunchback of Notre Dame, a red devil and a cowboy.

Janie's mother greeted us at the front door. The house had been completely transformed and decorated for Halloween with dim lights and scary music playing in the background.

"Where's your nun costume?"

Smart aleck Steven was directly behind me. I thought about responding with a snide comment but instead I ignored him. Janie was waiting for everyone inside. Without question she was adorable wearing a short blonde wig similar to the famous model, Twiggy. She wore a tight white turtleneck jersey that showed off her perky breasts, which only appeared within the last few months. With a very snug orange miniskirt and shiny white boots that went up to her knees, Janie could have just stepped out of a fashion magazine herself. I was shocked her mother allowed her to wear such a risqué costume.

The party was contained to Janie's spacious family room. Bowls of candy, potato chips and popcorn were displayed on several decorated tables. Mrs. McMack resembled Harriet Nelson wearing a crisp coral dress accessorized with pearls around her neck and a flowered apron was tied around her slim waist. As the woman scurried from the kitchen to the family room, bringing in more treats and beverages for everyone, a smile on her ruby red lips never left her face. She hummed to herself as she served apple cider from a beautiful crystal punch bowl.

We mingled and chatted about each other's costumes while Mrs. McMack set up the bobbing for apples game. We all took turns hovering over an aluminum pail of water while grabbing an apple with our front teeth.

"It's a good thing Bugsy isn't here!! She'd be chomping and biting all the apples!"

Everyone laughed at Steven's remark. But ultimately it was he who won the first place prize.

"Big surprise you won." I said sarcastically. The boy had the biggest mouth in class.

As we ate more snacks Mrs. McMack announced she would be out on the front porch if anyone needed anything. I looked out the picture window and watched as she rocked on the front porch swing, lit a cigarette and began to sip a drink out of a tall frosted glass. I wondered where Mr. McMack was. As soon as her mother left the room Janie gathered us around and whispered loudly, "Come here, come on! Follow me!"

It was if she had some big secret to tell. We were ushered to a smaller room just off the kitchen where Janie told us to sit down in a circle. There was only one small couch, a lamp and a console TV in the cramped space. Ellen and I glanced at one another then, under Janie's direction, sat next to one another on the linoleum floor.

"Are we telling ghost stories?" Francis asked, "Because I have some good ones."

"Just wait."

Janie could barely contain her excitement as she grinned from ear to ear. After she turned off the lamp she plopped down next to me. Her longs legs were folded underneath her, protecting anything under her skirt from showing. The room was extremely dark. Janie placed an empty bottle of Tab in the middle of our circle.

"Guess what we're playing?" she asked excitedly.

"Oh, I know what this is!" Steven said as he rubbed his palms together and grinned from ear to ear.

"Spin the bottle!"

Ellen and I looked at one another. Shit. I had to find a way out of this. I didn't want them to think I was scared but I had no desire to play that game especially with these boys. My mind raced as I tried to think of an excuse but nothing sounded good enough.

"That's right Steven! Is everybody ready? Since I'm the host I'll go first."

Without waiting for a response Janie spun the empty bottle round and round. It stopped and pointed directly at Patrick O'Sullivan.

Patrick began to squirm as he glanced around at everyone. It was obvious to me he had never played this game before either. Janie jumped up from the floor and held her hand out to the shy boy.

"C'mon Patrick! Now we have to go in the closet."

Patrick reluctantly stood. He was dressed as the Notre Dame hunchback and struggled for a bit with his cumbersome costume but I wondered if he was stalling to participate.

"Have fun, Pat!" Steven snickered as he and Francis began to laugh. I wanted to ask the two boys if they had experience with the game but was afraid of what I might find out. Patrick followed Janie into a closet just a few feet away. She opened the door and held her hand out to him, motioning for him to go inside. The hunchback shrugged his shoulders then did as he was told. Janie quietly shut the door.

"This is awkward" I whispered to Ellen. As the rest of us sat and waited I stared down at the floor. Wasn't Janie worried about her mother coming in?

From the family room, the creepy music continued to play in the background. It felt like hours but it was only a few minutes before the closet door reopened. Janie adjusted her wig then settled back down on the floor with a big smile on her face. Everyone looked up at Patrick who walked slowly back to our circle then sat down.

"So, how was it?" Steven elbowed him in the side.

"Alright." Patrick mumbled with his eyes downcast. The other boys chuckled. Steven rubbed his hands together and said, "Spin it somebody! I'm ready for a turn!"

Janie shoved the bottle in front of me. My heart pounded a bit as I took it and slowly placed it on the floor. Please, please God, let it land on Francis, I prayed.

I glanced over at Ellen with a concerned look then spun the bottle. It went round and round so fast before it came to a stop.

My heart dropped.

I closed my eyes and chewed on my bottom lip glad that it was dark in the room because my cheeks were getting hotter by the minute.

"Ooooh Mulldoon! It's your lucky day!"

Steven, dressed appropriately as a devil, jumped up from the floor. I cleared my throat then slowly got to my feet.

"Have fun kiddies!" Janie giggled. I was finding out that demure little Janie had a wild streak in her. As I tried to postpone the inevitable I thought of Mrs. McMack. I was desperate for any excuse.

"Janie, what about your mother?"

"Oh, don't worry about her. She's got her cigs and her whiskey highball. She'll be out for while."

The girl had all the answers.

I slowly made my way over to the closet where Steven was already waiting with the door open. He smiled and motioned for me to enter.

"I know, I know!" I said hesitantly.

The closet was completely dark. I had no idea how big the space was so I held out my hands to avoid walking into anything. I felt shelves along both sides before I stopped and turned around just when Steven shut the door. I couldn't see him or anything else.

"Well, well Maureen. Now it's just you and me."

I swallowed the lump in my throat and stood with my arms at my sides. When Steven reached out and touched my arm I jumped and whispered, "What are you doing!?"

"It's spin the bottle, dummy. What do you think we're going to do?"

My mind began to race.

"Okay, Steven. But only on the cheek. I mean it."

I waited.

I heard the rustle of his costume before I felt his breath on my face. I could smell Macintosh apples as he reached up with one hand and felt my cheek. Tingles ran up my spine. Why on earth was I feeling like this?

My mouth went dry and I was getting very warm. I turned my face to the right to make certain he kissed my cheek. But my aim was off. Before I knew it my nose bumped his nose. A quick brush of his lips swept across mine. For an instant our mouths were actually together and his lips felt very soft.

We separated and stood silent for what seemed like an eternity. I expected a smart ass comment but he never said a word. I tried to end the awkward situation.

"Okay, let's go. It's Ellen's turn to spin."

I gently pushed his arm as an indication to leave.

Steven opened the door and smiled as I passed.

The whole thing had not been as bad as I expected. But things with Steven were definitely different.

The following Monday I blushed when I met up with him in the classroom. I waited for his usual sarcastic greeting but he just looked at me with a silly grin. Sister Louise, who was standing at the doorway, looked first at Steven then at me.

That's when the guilt crept in.

I wondered if she could tell something had happened between us. Could she possibly know what we had done? By the end of the day I knew I had to go to confession.

And fast.

1971 GRADUATION

By spring of '71 our eighth grade class was prepared for graduation. It didn't seem possible that I would not be attending St. Timothy's the following September. My entire class chatted about leaving the confines of our school as some would be entering the public school system while others would continue on to a Catholic high school located fifty miles away. Ellen's parents had already informed her that she'd be riding a bus to the parochial school but I still didn't know where I would be attending, which caused some apprehension. I crossed my fingers each night as I listened to my parents discuss my future. Although I wanted to go with Ellen I knew the costly tuition of the Catholic high school could pose a problem. My father already worked several jobs and adding another monthly bill was nearly out of the question. They were dismayed and saddened to be torn between their religious devotion and the all important factor—money. For most of my eighth grade year my future remained up in the air as I waited anxiously for my parents' decision.

Groups of us huddled together every day at recess as we discussed our upcoming year at a new school. Almost all of my friends would be entering the public school system.

"I can't wait to escape these crows!"

"Those public school kids are wild! They can get away with anything!"

"Good riddance, Bugsy! No more Sister Bridgette!"

Of course I felt the same as the others but I had to admit I would miss the security of attending class with this same group of familiar faces. As I lay awake at night my thoughts always took over. If I were to attend the Catholic high school, I prayed the nuns would be different than those at St. Timothy's. I wondered how big the school was and if I would find my way. And the idea of riding a bus was intimidating as well. What if I missed it in the morning? What if I missed it after school? What if I didn't have any classes with Ellen? What if I don't make any friends? I had many sleepless nights.

At fourteen I was insecure about starting over. The nuns irritated me and I disliked all of their rules and silly admonitions but I knew St. Timothy's like the back of my hand. I could find my way through the building blindfolded. Most importantly, I knew which Sisters to steer clear of and which nuns I could trust.

And then there was the issue of my wardrobe. For eight years I'd worn school uniforms. I looked identical to the other girls, in plaid skirts, white blouses and knee socks. Neither the parochial high school nor the public school required uniforms which meant either way I needed a new clothes. Beginning in September I would have to think about what outfit to wear each day. And I needed to be sure it was up to date and not some plain homemade dress.

In May, Sister Louise arranged a field trip to the local high school. Several parents volunteered to drive us even though the school was just a short distance away on the shores of Lake Saukee. During the previous summer Ellen and I had ridden our bikes through the parking lot while on our way to the lake.

"It's so big! I can't imagine finding our classrooms."

I was overwhelmed by the size of the intimidating building. The far end of the school faced the water and as I looked up at the windows I wondered what lucky classroom had that spectacular view. We stopped and got off our bikes and walked them to the enormous front entrance. There were four double doors with large panels of glass in each. I put my hands up to a window and peered in. The corridor was three times the size of St. Timothy's front entrance. Long tables were placed just inside the doors. There was paper, file cards and pens stacked and ready for the first day of school. Beyond the tables was a row of lockers against the sea foam green walls.

"Hey, they have lockers. That'll be cool."

Ellen was trying to find something positive to say about the new school.

"It's better than carrying books around."

Our class field trip wasn't much help. As our group walked the halls students from the school made comments and laughed at us.

"Hey, look at those Catholic kids!"

"Where are the penguins?"

"Wow, cool uniforms, nerds!"

Their remarks were hurtful and made me nervous.

I felt like a foreigner.

Surprisingly, Steven kept his mouth shut when the boys were teasing. The school principal was friendly enough as he gave us a tour around the enormous facility. He showed us the area where freshmen orientation would be held and as we walked through the administrative office the secretary smiled and waved to us. He brought us to the huge cafeteria which resembled a restaurant. There were forty or so tables lined up with a serving line that ran across the length of one wall. I watched a dozen lunch ladies, wearing hair nets and dressed entirely in white, scurrying back and forth carrying large trays of food. One woman stood at the end of the line running the cash register. Next to the serving line were two glass cased freezers. Students purchased ice cream sandwiches and other treats. No one was monitoring them. There was no adults approaching the tables and correcting their table manners. The atmosphere was much different than the small cafeteria at St. Timothy's. The noisy room was very active while trays and silverware clanged and students shouted over the blaring music from a juke box. The principal had to speak up as he talked over the noise.

"Cool! They have music!" Steven shouted. "This isn't such a bad deal."

Yeah, it was cool. But music or no music I still felt uneasy as I observed the students. Everyone was dressed in fashionable outfits. Groups of girls giggled and pointed at us as we walked through. Suddenly two boys, who looked like much older than us, began to argue loudly at a table close by. When they began to throw fists at each other out of nowhere a man, perhaps a teacher, stepped up to the table and separated the two boys. By now, one had a bloody nose. As the principal ran over to help he grabbed a walkie-talkie and began to speak into it. Then the other man took each boy by the arm and escorted them out of the cafeteria. I looked over at Steven who was expressionless. The whole incident had been a bit unnerving. Nothing like that had ever happened at St. Timothy's.

The tour concluded with a walk through the gigantic gymnasium then outside to the running track where most of our physical education would be held. We were told it was mandatory to wear uniforms to class. I wondered what they were like because we didn't wear gym uniforms at St. Timothy's. It was, however, the only day of the week the nuns allowed girls to wear slacks and the boys were allowed to wear shorts. Everything was very different here.

After making our way back to the front entrance the principal handed a small packet to each of us. Inside was a sheet outlining all of the required freshman classes, a list of rules and regulations for us to follow and recommended supplies to purchase.

That night as I lay in bed and went over the entire day I had to keep telling myself it would be okay, that I wasn't the only one afraid to start at the new school.

The following day everyone was buzzing about the field trip.

"Did you see what those girls were wearing? We definitely have some shopping to do!"

Sister Louise clapped her hands to get our attention.

"Class! Pay attention! We need to go over the graduation ceremony."

She handed out envelopes and forms to order our cap and gown.

It was becoming real.

There had been a lot of talk amongst the nuns regarding our class since we were the last eighth grade class to graduate from St. Timothy's. Changes were being made after 80 years of functioning on their own. In September St. Timothy's would merge with two other parochial schools from the surrounding area. Enrollment had decreased in each of the schools due to high tuition costs and the diocese decided it best to combine them and limit the grade level to fifth grade. It was a major blow to the nuns and the Catholic school community.

Sister Bridgette's voice cracked over the intercom system as she announced the news.

"This year is a solemn one at St. Timothy's. It will be the end of an era."

There was a long pause as she sniffed her nose.

"Next September we will no longer be known as St. Timothy's"

She cleared her throat and continued.

"The new name will be Trinity Academy."

We looked at one another as Sister Louise blew her nose and turned her back to us.

"We wish our last graduating class of 1971 the best of luck in the future. God bless you all."

Changes were quickly happening.

"Since this is to be a special occasion for St. Timothy's the diocese is sending Bishop Philip to say mass for us."

Sister Louise announced to us one morning as she handed out instructions to give to our parents, who would be assisting in the graduation celebration. My mother, along with Ellen's was on the list to provide decorations.

"Please remind your parents of the upcoming committee meeting next week." Sister said.

"Where's the big party going to be?"

Steven received a menacing look from the nun.

"Mr. O'Hara, we will be having a cordial, a nice function, if you will, down in the cafeteria."

Within a few weeks Mr. Lachant delivered a huge box to our classroom. Inside were dark green satin gowns with similar graduation caps adorned with a gold tassel. Each was individually wrapped in plastic with our name on an outside label. The classroom was buzzing with anticipation as we tore the bags open and tried them on. It took some time for Sister to quell our excitement as she instructed us to fold them neatly and take them home.

Ellen and I had a lot to talk about on the way home that day. We made plans to go to O'Shea's department store the following Saturday. Both of us needed new dresses for graduation but most importantly for the party afterward. O'Shea's was pricier than Woolworth's or JJ Newberry's but it was the only place in town to get the most current style. We planned to work on our hairstyles too as we wanted to look like graduates and not just Catholic school girls.

After finishing chores one Saturday afternoon Ellen and I walked downtown to Main Street. We immediately went to the junior department at O'Shea's where a shipment of new spring styles had just arrived.

My heart sunk.

All of the bright colors and florals clashed with my hair. After a lot of searching I finally found a pale lilac dress that was perfect. I dug into my change purse and pulled out the babysitting money I had saved over the last several months.

Next stop—hosiery. Ellen and I had talked about this for weeks.

We giggled as we headed over to that department and looked at the different garter belts that were available. There were a lot of choices and so many varieties of nylons.

I was deep in thought while trying to choose a size when I heard a familiar voice behind me.

"Miss Mulldooooon. Where do youuuuu intend on wearing thoooose!?"

I cringed. There was no mistaking Bugsy's voice.

"Hello, Sister. Um, well I thought I'd wear nylons for graduation."

I looked up to find her glaring at the two of us as she leaned over the display case. She looked exactly as she did at school. The only difference was she carried a small black purse. I wondered what she could possibly be shopping for since she was hidden under that dreary black habit.

"Miss Mulldoon, you know perfectly well that nylon hose is not acceptable. I suggest you choose a nice pair of knee socks."

"Yes Sis-"

Before I could finish my sentence the nun turned and marched off to the shoe department.

My friend and I watched the surly woman walk away.

"Nasty old crow, she still has a mean streak in her." Ellen whispered.

I had to agree. I had hoped the nun had softened over the years. Something about Bugsy intrigued me and I wondered what caused her to lash out at people the way she did.

With the help of a nice sales clerk Ellen and I chose new garter belts and tan nylons, to cover our pasty white legs. She assured us of the sizes and I was excited to wear them. With the perfect dress and stockings and a new pair of white sandals my mother bought me I felt prepared for graduation. I also bought an arsenal of hair products to ensure a hip and up to date look that night.

Several times a week Sister Louise brought us down to the gym and we lined up, two by two. Thankfully, our placement was done by height so I was able to walk with the girls. Even though Sister Louise was directing the processional, Sister Bridgette had her hands in it as well.

"Quiet students! Quiet! With all of your chatter you will not hear Sister Louise's instructions."

If she had a whip she probably would have snapped it.

"Why is Bugsy always stickin' her nose in stuff?" Steven asked quite loudly.

"Do you have something to say Mr. O'Hara?"

He hadn't realized she was standing right behind him.

Steven shook his head. "No Sister"

In recent weeks Sister Bridgette had started to mellow. Maybe it was old age or maybe she was just tired of us but her demeanor towards me had changed as well. She even said good morning to me most mornings when I passed her in the hall. I sensed a change in her but I just couldn't figure out what it was. Every now and then she reverted back to her wicked ways and lashed out with her sharp tongue but there was softness to her as well.

The evening of graduation I took a bubble bath and put on my new dress, nylons and shoes. Thankfully my curls were tamed and manageable. With tons of bobby pins and hairspray I was able to maintain the current shag hairstyle. My mother did not allow me to wear makeup but at least I was able to shave my armpits and legs.

My parents, siblings and grandparents waited just outside of church. The school driveway was lined with cars as they forged their way to the parking lot. People were everywhere. It was a big occasion for our school, our parish and our community. I found Ellen in the gym and slipped on my cap and gown.

There was excitement in the air as Mr. Lachant put finishing touches on the stage and Sister Bridgette barked out orders. The poor guy was scrambling to make things perfect. One hundred or so folding chairs were placed in rows facing the stage. Fresh flowers and gold and white balloons adorned each corner of the stage. A podium was placed in the center and chairs were set up for our graduating class to the right of that. A large banner that read, 'Congratulations Graduates' hung across the stage backdrop.

At promptly 6:00 pm Sister Bridgette waved her arm high above her head to get our attention as she walked the length of the gym. Lined up and ready to go we proceeded over to church. It was breezy outside and I had to hang onto my cap and tassel.

The church was packed with hundreds of people that had come to witness the last graduating class of St. Timothy's. Flash bulbs went off as we slowly processed down the middle aisle to the organist's music of *Praise to the Lord, the Almighty*. I trembled as my eyes scanned the church. There were so many people there I struggled to find my family. Then I saw a white gloved hand waving frantically in the air. It belonged to my mother. I managed a small smile, but that was it, this was supposed to be a serious occasion. Sister would kill me if she caught me waving to the crowd. A shrill whistle suddenly came from my right. I glanced over and saw a tall redheaded high school boy standing on the kneeler with two fingers in his opened mouth. How dare he whistle in church! There was no doubt he was related to Steven because he looked exactly like him. Steven, who was just behind my partner, smiled and waved at the boy and all the other redheads that were lined up in the same pew. So, that's what his family looked like.

I turned my attention to the procession and looked ahead at the altar. The table was lit with candles in the front corners and vases of flowers decorated the area. Bishop Philip stood in front of the red velvet chair as we continued down the aisle. He was surrounded by several altar boys and Father Murphy stood to his side. The bishop held a large wooden staff that resembled a walking stick. We filed into our pews located right in front of the altar. To our left, on the opposite side of the aisle, were all of the nuns that taught us at St. Timothy's. Sister Dympna, Sister Cornelius, Sister Oliver, Sister Alexander, Sister Claire and Sister Bridgette sat in the front row. Sister Xavier was said to be too ill to attend. Sister Louise took her place at the end of that row once we were all seated.

With the glow from the candles and the fresh smell of incense mass felt very special. It was surreal to think that from that night on I would have no connection with the nuns across the way. All of those years of being scared, intimidated and ridiculed were now behind me. I felt free. Free to speak up, free from their ever present criticizing eyes and hopefully free from any more guilt. I didn't anticipate the same sort of treatment at the new school where the teachers were regular people, lay teachers they called them. I was sure they couldn't be as mean.

Once communion was over we waited for the signal from Bishop Philip. We stood when he stood.

I felt my garter snap. The front clip had popped off causing my hose to slowly creep down my thigh. I swallowed hard as my mind raced to think of a way to stop it. I tried to pinch a bit of the nylon by holding on to the fabric of my graduation gown but discovered that would never work as I'd have to hold it all the way out of church. I hoped and prayed the garter clip on the back of my thigh stayed put. And I was grateful that the gown went down to my ankles.

The bishop's blessing was lengthy as he went on and on about the legacy of St. Timothy's. I couldn't remember half of what he said as I concentrated on the fabric that was slowly slipping down my leg.

The nylon was stretched on the back of my thigh but stayed connected until we returned to school. Our class congregated in the stairwell as parents and family members made their way to their seats. I desperately wanted to go to the lavatory to fix the problem but Sister Bridgette would not allow it. She was frantic as she scurried about making sure everything was going according to plan. She nudged Father Murphy who was leaning out the side door, flicking the remains of a well smoked cigarette.

"Father, we haven't much time, please get to the stage."

He grunted and mumbled as he went down the stairs to take his place; the lingering odor of a Lucky Strike trailed behind him.

"Shhhhhhh!"

She was trying her best to keep us quiet so we could hear the announcement from the stage.

I could hear Sister Claire's voice over the loud speakers.

"Attention! Quiet please!" She struggled to get the crowd to settle down. "Hello!"

Once she began to play *The Pomp and Circumstance March* on the piano the crowd quieted and we proceeded to the gym.

Everyone was silent as we marched in. By now the sun had set and the gym had a soft glow from the stage lights. My eyes began to water. I couldn't stop the tears and tried to compose myself by biting my bottom lip. As we filed onto the stage and took our places, Sister Bridgette stood at the podium.

"Good evening everyone. Tonight is a very, very, special occasion. This class, class of 1971, is the final one to graduate from what is now known as St. Timothy's Catholic School."

She held out her hand and motioned to where we sat. There was a light applause.

"Words cannot describe what the other Sisters and myself are feeling tonight. We've taught each and every one of these students for most of their eight years."

She paused and wiped her nose. It appeared that Bugsy was getting emotional.

"We hope we have instilled in each of them the love of Christ. And we pray that each of them will continue with their strong faith and remain faithful to the church."

This time she lifted her glasses and wiped her eyes.

I looked over at Ellen who mouthed to me 'is she crying?' I shrugged my shoulders.

"There were times when our patience was tried, of course. But I feel the tradition of our schooling has taught them the respect that is needed to continue on in their high school years and beyond."

"Yeah, they showed us alright. I have the scars to prove it!" Steven whispered loudly. I chuckled even though it wasn't funny. Each of us would be walking away with vivid memories of the nuns' cruel punishments.

"And now it's time for the awards. I'd like to welcome our pastor, Father Philip Murphy."

The audience applauded as Father Murphy shuffled to the podium and continually pushed his glasses back onto the bridge of his nose. Sister Bridgette stood to one side.

"I hope he doesn't spit all over the diplomas." Steven said above the noise. Father began with an opening prayer before Sister handed him a sheet of paper.

He announced the names of students receiving awards. Some received a Certificate of Merit while others received an award for having all A's on their report card. I knew I'd never get one of those. My report cards consisted of B's and C's, at best with an occasional A in English.

"Receiving a Certificate of Merit is Maureen Mary Mulldoon."

Someone nudged me on the shoulder. I never expected to hear my name. I slowly walked to the podium forgetting all about my sagging nylon, which thankfully still held on. I heard a loud applause and looked out to see my Dad. He stood tall and proud, with a big smile under his handlebar moustache. I smiled back at him and returned to my seat.

After diplomas were handed out alphabetically we returned to our seats when Patrick stood to recite paragraphs from President Kennedy's famous inaugural speech. I thought back to third grade when he had gotten into trouble with Steven and wet his pants in front of everyone. I believe he learned his lesson more than Steven had, because he never got into that kind of trouble again.

Sister Bridgette announced the next speaker. There was a light applause as Janie stepped up to the podium. Not the least bit bashful, the prissy girl dramatically adjusted the microphone before she began.

"Thank you, thank you."

It was as though she were already the actress she hoped to become. She must have practiced her verse from the bible, a letter to St Timothy; because she spoke slowly and dramatized the entire thing. I looked over at Sister Bridgette, who was beaming with pride as though she were Janie's mother.

Afterwards, Sister Louise stepped up to the podium. She didn't have any notes with her. Sister cleared her throat and began by thanking Father Murphy, Sister Bridgette and Sister Claire for their involvement in the graduation ceremony. There was a long pause as the entire room went silent.

Then Sister softly addressed each one of us. She thanked us for being her students. And then she did something I never forgot. She reflected on something positive about each one of her graduates.

"Maureen, you've come a long way. You are becoming more and more self confident, an intelligent young lady. Don't let anyone tell you otherwise."

I felt a lump in my throat. Sister had really seen us as real people, not just subjects who sat in her classroom. She didn't just stand up there and teach. She came to know each one of us individually.

"Steven O'Hara, what can I say?"

A light ripple of laughter trickled throughout the gym before a loud whistle screeched from the back row.

One of Steven's brothers stood to honor his younger sibling.

"Oh, I could probably tell a few good stories about you, but I won't. I will say that you have matured into a nice young man. Please keep it that way. You'll go a long way in life."

Steven actually looked embarrassed as he smiled and shrugged his shoulders.

When she was through she wished us well and Father Murphy returned to say the final prayer.

The entire gymnasium recited in unison "In the name of the Father, and of the Son and of the Holy Ghost, Amen."

As we began to leave the stage we received a standing ovation from our families. Sister Bridgette breathed heavily into the microphone as she tried to make an announcement.

"Students! Students! Please deposit your caps and gowns behind the stage please. Then you may proceed to the cafeteria for refreshments."

I made my way quickly to the back, dropped off the cap and gown and immediately went to the lavatory to fix my garter.

I made it just in time.

1971 THE LAST DANCE

Ellen met me inside the lavatory and after a simple garter fix we hurried to the cafeteria, excited for the party. I was amazed when I saw the transformed lunch room. Silver streamers shimmered in the dim lighting while white and gold balloons were anchored on each of the covered tables. Hundreds of star shaped cut outs dangled from the ceiling. It felt like we were under the stars. The old lunch tables were covered with navy blue tablecloths and had been moved to the outer edges of the room creating a huge dance floor in the middle. Current hit tunes played loudly from a record player located near the serving line. The room was magical.

"Wow, this is super cool!"

Everyone was pleasantly surprised as they entered the cafeteria. It didn't feel like a Catholic school anymore. Across the room I saw Steven and some of the other boys digging into the bowls of chips placed on the tables. There were no nuns in the room but a few parents observed from the kitchen. One of the mothers approached us.

"Come on in girls! There are plenty of drinks, sandwiches and snacks on the tables."

She pointed to two large coolers packed with ice and soda. There were bottles of Tab, Coca Cola, Orange Crush and Pepsi Cola to choose from. Trays filled with homemade finger sandwiches looked tempting but I was too excited to eat. Ellen and I took sodas and found seats with the other girls.

Across the room Francis and Steven threw pieces of popcorn at one another. Janie was alone on the dance floor dancing to *One Bad Apple* by The Osmonds. I shook my head and laughed. Not at her in particular but because she just didn't care who was watching. When the Three Dog Night song began to play I threw caution to the wind and joined Janie on the dance floor. One by one other girls joined us.

"Joy to the world, all the boys and girls!"

Together we laughed and danced without a care. The boys stood off to the side watching us. Steven and his friends pointed and snickered, but it didn't matter. It was my last night at St. Timothy's and I was determined to enjoy it. Eventually two of the parents decided to join us as well.

When the music changed to a slow ballad everyone left the dance floor. Ellen and I sat at one of the table while The Carpenters sang *For All We Know*. I could see the boys out of the corner of my eye and secretly wished they would ask one of us to dance. I spotted Francis, standing alone drinking a soda. He was even more handsome in his navy sports jacket and striped tie. Unfortunately he didn't appear to be the least bit interested in dancing. And I knew it would be too brazen for me to ask him.

The night went by quickly and we were enjoying a lot of laughs. The girls dominated the dance floor the entire evening. The only nun to stop by was Sister Claire who stood and chatted with the chaperones. During the time she was there I observed her as she swayed to the music. She was such a pretty nun and again I wondered why she would want to give up a life of dancing and boys. I suppose she had her reasons but I never understood. But I did know one thing—becoming a nun was not a vocation for me.

Towards the end of the evening the girls and I were tired of dancing with one another and began to sit out most of the songs.

Then *My Sweet Lord* by George Harrison began to play. I absolutely loved the song and the lyrics. I leaned back in my chair, closed my eyes and began to sing.

There was a tap on my shoulder. When I looked up I almost choked on my popcorn. Steven held out his hand as he reached for mine. I hesitated. Was this one of his pranks? I looked around him and then up at his face. He was certainly different, more serious. I let him take my hand and he slowly led me onto the dance floor. With his eyes never leaving mine I never even noticed if the others watching us.

The music played on as he held me just as he did when we danced in the Christmas pageant a year before. His palms were clammy but for some reason this time I didn't care. My heart was pounding and I felt dizzy.

I forgot all about Francis.

George Harrison's voice filled the room. Steven put his cheek against the side of my head. I closed my eyes as we slowly danced in a tiny circle. We didn't move much, just round and round until the song ended. I felt very warm inside and knew my cheeks were probably glowing. Relieved when another fast song began to play, I glanced around to see that Ellen had been slow dancing with Francis and Janie with Patrick. Steven continued to hold my hand and led us to two secluded seats in the corner. Again I wondered if anyone were watching us but this time I didn't care. Steven turned his chair and we sat face to face. I gulped, not knowing what to expect from him. Just then the lights came on in the cafeteria.

Students began to leave for home and parents began to clean up.

"Mulldoon—I mean Maureen," he fidgeted in his chair. "I just want to tell you… I'm sorry."

"For what?"

I instinctively removed my hand from his, afraid of what he was about to tell me. Knowing Steven, I wondered if he was playing me for a fool or this was some kind of a joke.

"Wait a minute, hear me out."

The look on his face told me it wasn't a joke.

"I just want to apologize for all the hurtful things I've ever said or done to you."

He seemed genuinely ashamed as he cast his eyes to the floor.

"I know I was hurtful and you didn't deserve any of it."

I never expected this, but it felt good. I had no idea how to responds so I remained silent and let him talk.

"I don't know why I said those things and teased you calling you gopher and goon. But I'm really sorry."

I had no choice but to accept his apology and forgive. After all, that's what we had been taught for the last eight years. I reached over and gently laid a hand on his arm.

As we strolled in silence through the gym I thought about asking which school he would be attending in the fall, but I just didn't have the courage. When it was too quiet between us I punched him lightly on the arm in jest.

"Ow, what's that for?"

He laughed and rubbed his arm.

"You owe me!"

I felt myself blushing but continued anyway. I turned to face him.

"I challenge you to a game of marbles. Let's meet this Saturday—that's if you're not scared."

"Aw, Jesus, come on, Maureen! Goddamn it, you know you'll beat me, you always do!"

Just as we climbed the stairs to head outside we met up with Bugsy who was standing on the landing.

"Mr. O'Hara, I suggest you watch your language in the presence of a lady!"

"Yes, Sister."

We hurried past the nun and just made it out the door before bursting into laughter. Before I knew it he was holding my hand again as we chatted and decided on a time to meet. I looked around the playground and felt a tinge of sadness. So many memories came flooding back, some happy and some I would rather forget.

As we strolled slowly down the driveway and headed to Main Street a piece of paper blew under my feet.

I scooped it up and sighed. It was one of our graduation programs.

I folded it and kept it as a memory.

It was one of many I saved from St. Timothy's Catholic School.

1st Holy Communion

Rosary case

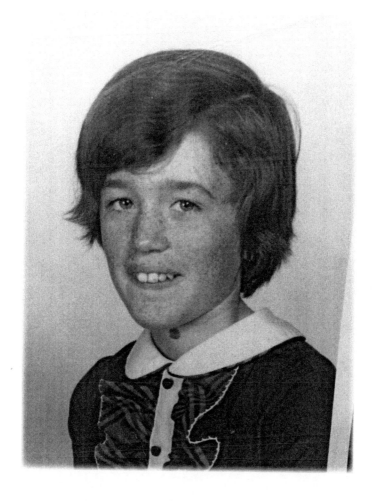

7th Grade picture

My best friend

Diocese of Manchester

REPORT OF PUPIL PROGRESS

GRADES 3 through 8

School ....

Pupil ....

Grade .... September, 19.66 to June, 19.67.

Teacher ...... *Sister M. Cornelius, RSM* ......

TO THE PARENTS OR GUARDIANS,

This report is an important message from teacher to parents. Please read it carefully. The marks are the teacher's account of your child's academic progress and school behavior.

If you have any doubts or questions about these marks, please arrange with the school principal for an interview, outside of school hours, with your child's teacher.

You are required to sign this report card. Your signature does not indicate that you are satisfied in every instance with the conduct and achievement of your child, but it does give

Report Card

Bugsy and Me

Class picture - the bird

Graduation and our priest

CPSIA information can be obtained at www.ICGtesting.com
Printed in the USA
LVOW080308170513

334262LV00001B/4/P

9 781452 573465